The Man Who Came Back

When, as a scrawny kid, Jack Slade ran from Blake's Creek because they had lynched his pa for a crime he didn't commit, the boy vowed to come back one day and get his revenge. Many moons later Jack finally did return and met up with a feisty newspaperwoman by the name of Clara Lezard. Her father had been killed by the same man who was responsible for the lynching of Slade's father. Now there were two formidable characters bent on revenge.

There was much killing to be done before the whole matter could be settled and Jack's gun skills would be fully tested in the harrowing showdown.

The Man Who Came Back

BRENDAN FAGAN

A Black Horse Western

ROBERT HALE · LONDON

© Brendan Fagan 2003
First published in Great Britain 2003

ISBN 0 7090 7336 4

Robert Hale Limited
Clerkenwell House
Clerkenwell Green
London EC1R 0HT

Typeset by
Derek Doyle & Associates, Liverpool.
Printed and bound in Great Britain by
Antony Rowe Limited, Wiltshire

ONE

When Jack Slade rode down the dusty street nobody took much notice of him, and those that did notice him didn't seem to remember him. When he left he had been a scrawny fourteen-year-old kid, undersized and undernourished, and pretty timid. Now he was a man in his mid-thirties, a foot taller and a foot broader. With some notches on his gun.

He had restless eyes and a tied-down gun at his hip. He didn't know why he had come back. There had been nothing in Blake's Creek since the day his ma had told him that his pa was going to be dragged out of the jail and lynched for a crime he was innocent of, and that they were coming for his son next.

He had run from the cabin, straight to the edge of town with no clear idea of what he was going to do, but that didn't matter. At the last minute, with no clear plan or idea, his courage had failed him, and in the dark, he had run and hidden under the boardwalk of the saloon. He had watched speechless with terror as his pa had been dragged out of the jail. A jail strangely empty of a sheriff and his deputies.

His pa had kicked and fought all the way to the tree while one of the men pulled the noose over his neck and tightened it. Then they had hoisted him on to the horse and fired a shot that stampeded it, and left his pa kicking, his eyes bulging, his tongue lolling out of his mouth. It seemed to take him all night to stop kicking at the empty air, but then he did, and his body just hung there, swinging gently in the growing light of a new day.

Before all the townsfolk had gone home, Jack Slade had crawled through the boardwalk to the back of the saloon, then started running. He ran until he could run no more and fell exhausted into the hot dust.

A woman's voice had woken him up, a harsh strident voice that was seldom lower than a rasping bawl. Her thin face seemed always to have a harsh scowl on it.

'He still alive?' he could remember her shouting as he opened his eyes and looked up into Jethro's face.

'Yuh, he's alive, but it ain't by much though,' Jethro yelled, pouring some water from his canteen on to his bandanna.

He wiped the bandanna across Slade's face. Then he put the canteen to the boy's lips and gently tipped it so that no more than a drop ran over the edge on to the boy's lips. Slade's swollen tongue licked greedily at it, then sought some more.

'Go easy on that water, Jethro,' the woman's voice called out. 'Give him too much an' yer likely to make him sicker than he is.'

'Take it easy, Martha,' Jethro retorted under his breath. 'I'm doing the best I can for him.'

'Git him in the wagon, it's gonna be real hot before too long, an' that won't help him any.'

Slade had felt Jethro's strong hands lifting him out of the dust and carrying him over to the old wagon. As Jethro put him down on the mattress, Slade had felt the relief from the rising heat outside. He saw the woman for the first time and guessed that she must be Jethro's wife. She was the same age as Jethro, but her face was older and had more lines in it. She had her grey hair tied back in a tight bun behind her head, her eyes were kindly and made Slade feel right at home.

'Where am I?' Slade gasped; his tongue still felt thick and swollen.

'Where yer safe,' Martha replied, stroking his head, the scowl still on her face, but softening a mite. 'Don't you worry any more. Whoever's after you won't get you here.'

The wagon lurched on for a spell, with Slade sleeping through a nightmare that haunted him through the day and early evening. He was awake when the wagon finally stopped and he could hear Jethro climb down from the seat up top. The wagon lurched as he climbed inside. A minute later a freshening breeze licked his face as Jetro opened the flap. His hands lifted him from the old mattress and he carried him into a small cabin and laid him on to a hard bed. Later Jethro told him that he had slept for two days after that. By the third day he was well enough to get out of the bed, and hobble around on a pair of crutches that Jethro fixed up for him out of some tree saplings. Then there were days when he rebuilt his strength and got to help Martha round the cabin, while Jethro was out getting the cook-pot filled up with anything he could get in the sights of his hunting rifle.

'Martha says you can get around without them sticks I fixed up fer you,' Jethro said one night while they were sitting out on the step of the cabin.

'My feet are just about healed up,' Slade said, watching a shooting star peel across the sky, leaving a trail of fire behind it.

'Maybe tomorrow you'd care to come up into the woods with me. I'll teach you to shoot, and that'll be more for the pot. And maybe if you've a mind you could go back where you came from and settle a few scores sometime.'

Slade gave him a questioning look when he said this.

'Oh, I know all about yer pa, and the way they

strung him up. You said the helluva lot while you were rambling about in yer head,' Jethro said sympathetically, as he still whittled away at a piece of wood in his gnarled hands.

It was the first time that it occurred to Slade that he might have said anything, and he was glad that it was out in the open. A shudder ran through his thin frame.

'I ain't sayin' you should go back an' kill these fellas, but the Lord would understand if you did,' Jethro said, still whittling at the piece of wood.

'I reckon he might and that would be a good idea,' Slade replied, watching the sky above him.

For the first time for he could not remember how long, he slept without the nightmares. When he woke in the morning, the first thing he noticed was that his appetite had returned with a vengeance. Martha watched in surprise as he emptied his plate, and looked up for some more. Half an hour later they were following the narrow trail up the side of the mountain. Jethro had given him his spare rifle, and was leading the way, his eyes on the ground. He put up his hand to stop Slade coming any further, then he signalled him to follow him. When Slade caught up he hunkered down and followed the direction of Jethro's pointing finger. A few yards away a pair of deer were feeding on the thin grass.

Jethro raised his rifle and curled his finger round the trigger. A second later the sound of the shot echoed through the clearing. The deer that Jethro had fired at jumped a little and fell. It's mate was already running away down the mountainside.

Slade raised his gun, but Jethro put his hand on it and pushed it down.

'It's out of range. You'd just be wasting ammunition, and ammunition's hard to come by hereabouts.'

Slade felt disappointed that Jethro had not let him fire at the deer, but he realized that Jethro was right. The deer was half-way down the mountain before he could even get a bead on it. Jethro showed him how to skin the stricken deer once they had got it back to the cabin. Martha watched with satisfaction as Jethrro showed Slade how to go about it.

'I'm real glad that you and Jethro are getting on; it's been hard for him out here since our boy died. Near killed him.'

What Martha had said took Slade by surprise. He had never thought of them having children of their own.

'Took you by surprise, didn't it?' Martha asked him, a thoughtful look crossing her face.

For a moment, Slade didn't answer, then he said, 'Yes, I guess it did.'

'He'd just about started walking when he sneaked out of the cabin one day. Jethro found him later. He reckoned a bear had got him. At least it was quick.'

Her voice broke and she rushed into the cabin, leaving Slade to finish cleaning up the mess. The next day neither Jethro nor Martha mentioned anything about the boy. Nor ever again.

The next day they went up into the mountain again and filled the pot. Jethro showed Slade how to aim the gun and squeeze the trigger, but there was no ammunition in the rifle.

'Now take it real slow,' Jethro told him. 'You ain't got all day exactly, but you've got to take some time.'

They went through it time after time until Slade had got it right and Jethro was satisfied with him. He showed Slade how to track and showed him the difference between the tracks each animal left, and where they liked to feed.

'We're gonna have to go down the mountain tomorrow,' Jethro said after supper. 'We're getting low on ammunition, and some of the stuff I use to make my own needs replacing. We'll be starting out real early.'

The following morning they started off down the mountain again. They camped at a dried-out river-bed on the first night, and by the edge of a wooded area the next night. By first light the next day they were there.

'Place called Flaxton,' Jethro told Slade, who was riding up front with him. Martha was in the wagon, resting from the sun. She hadn't been feeling too good for a couple of days. Slade and

Jethro were beginning to worry about her.

Flaxton wasn't a big place, just a hole in the wall that might grow into something some day. Jethro swung down from the wagon. Slade followed him, and waited while he looked at Martha.

'She's gonna be fine fer a spell,' Jethro said when he came back. Slade thought Jethro wasn't telling him the whole truth. 'What say we wet our whistles. There's a place over there where they serve warm beer, but it is beer.' Jethro pointed to a saloon across the dusty street.

'Can't think why we shouldn't,' Slade said with a grin.

Together they crossed the street and pushed in through the batwing doors. The place was full, and Jethro tossed a few greetings to some of the folks in there. He sidled up to the bar and ordered a couple of beers. When they came he dropped the coins in the barkeep's hands and took the head off his beer. Slade took his a little slower. He'd never had strong drink before.

'Just enjoy it,' Jethro told him. 'I'll see you don't get into any trouble.'

'Thanks,' Slade said with a grin as he wiped the foam off his lips.

By the time they had had a couple more Slade was beginning to feel the effects of the beer.

'Best make that the last 'til you've gotten used to it,' Jethro said with a grin.

'I think you're right,' Slade said, his speech a little slurred. He felt hot and a mite dizzy.

Jethro guided him to the door and stood in the fresh air until he felt better.

'I've got to take a leak,' Slade said suddenly, clutching at his trouser-front.

Jethro guided him to the corner of the alley. 'This is as good a place as any,' he said, pushing Slade further into the alley.

Once out of sight Slade unbuttoned his trousers and took his leak. As he was buttoning up he heard the sounds of an argument from further down the alley. A man and woman were quarrelling violently.

Slade's head was swimming from the drink. Without thinking he ran down the alley towards the sound of the argument. The woman, he could see, was one of the soiled doves from the saloon. The man she was arguing with he reckoned was her customer.

'Give me my wallet,' the man yelled, trying to pull something from the whore's hands.

'You go straight to hell. I know you was trying to get away without paying me,' she yelled loudly.

The man swung his fist to hit her in her face, but Slade caught his hand and pulled him away from the girl.

'Leave her alone,' Slade shouted at him.

The man reeled back against the side of the building, his face turning purple with rage.

'You little bastard,' he yelled at Slade, his hand darting for the knife in the scabbard behind his back.

It came out, its point glinting. Slade crouched to meet the man's rush, but Jethro had come down the alley and flung himself between them. He and the girl's attacker hit the ground, but Jethro was lithe and fast, and pretty fit. He was on his feet quicker than the other man. His fist crashed into the purple face, squashing the nose. The girl screamed shrilly as her attacker went down. She screamed again as the alley started to fill up with people. One of them was wearing a star.

'He tried to get away without paying for his fun,' the girl said to the sheriff.

'Yeah, it's OK, Millie. He's tried it on with the other girls a couple of times. Just don't like paying for it, do you, Milt?'

Milt held his hand to stop the blood flowing, and mumbled something incoherently.

'You fellas OK?' the sheriff said, turning to Jethro and Slade once he had got the man's arm up his back.

'This young fella saved me an' my money,' Millie said, rushing to Slade's side and holding on to his arm.

'It was more Jethro than me,' Slade said quickly, realizing that he was blushing as the girl spoke.

'It doesn't matter who it was,' the sheriff said.

'I'll let you sort that out between yourselves.' He started to push his prisoner through the crowd to the jail.

Slade and the others watched them go.

'I guess I ought to show you fellas my appreciation for what you did,' Millie said, taking hold of Slade's and Jethro's arms.

'There's no need for that,' Jethro said quickly as he drew free of the girl. 'I think maybe my young friend would benefit more from it than I would, besides I'm a married man.'

'What did he mean by that?' Slade asked in a puzzled way.

'I'll show you what he means by that,' Millie said, dragging him into the saloon.

'Sobered up yet?' Jethro asked him with a grin when Slade came back to the wagon.

Slade blushed, and gave a sheepish grin.

'Yeah, I've sobered up, and how.'

'Well it had to happen sometime,' Jethro said, slapping him on the shoulder.

'I guess so,' Slade said with a laugh.

They spent a couple of days in town without Martha seeming to get better, then on the third day her fever worsened. The sweat poured off her thin face, and her eyes rolled wildly. Slade and Jethro took her to the doctor's office and waited while he examined her. From the look on his face they knew that it was bad.

'Maybe if you'd have got her to me sooner,' he

said, 'I might have been able to do something for her, but it's too late now, the sickness has gone too far.'

'You sure, Doc?' Jethro asked pleadingly.

'Positive,' the doctor said with an air of finality.

Jethro's face dropped. 'There's nothing you can do for her?' he almost pleaded.

'No, nothing. She's in a coma now, and I don't think she's going to wake up. I'm sorry,' the doc said.

They buried her three days later. Slade and Jethro stood alone under a tree watching the gravediggers fill in the hole.

'What'll you do now?' Slade asked, as they walked down to where the wagon stood.

Jethro said nothing for a minute. 'I guess I was kinda hoping you'd come back with me, but it doesn't look it's gonna be that way, does it.'

'Guess not,' Slade told him. 'There's a heap of places I've got to go, and a heap of things I've got to do.'

'You mean like going back to where you came from, and settling up for your pa?'

'I think maybe I will go back, but not yet,' Slade told him.

Jethro stuck out his hand. 'I guess I'll be seein' you, then.'

Slade took the hand and held it for a moment. 'Thanks for everything you've done.'

Jethro climbed into the wagon and put the

whip across the backs of the horses. Slade watched him go until he had disappeared down the trail.

It was the last time that Slade ever saw him.

TWO

'Seems like you'll be lookin' for a job,' a voice behind him said.

Slade turned and found himself looking at the sheriff.

'Smart piece of work you did that night. I've been watching you,' the sheriff went on. 'Seem like the kind of fella a sheriff might find useful in a tight fix.'

By the time Ben Jackson had walked him down to the office, Slade found himself agreeing that he had always wanted to be a lawman.

Ben bought him a gun from the town funds and showed him how to use it.

'It's a heap different from using a rifle,' he told Slade when Slade said he knew how to shoot.

They had been out to the river one day. When they had finished Ben took his gun from him and reloaded it.

'You've got to get close up to the fella you've

got a beef with. He's got to know he's gonna get hurt as well.'

After a while he said, 'Can't teach you any more about shooting.' He gave Slade back his gun.

Then they took the trail back to town. When they got back, Slade and Ben knew straight away that something was wrong. There was a crowd round the bank. As they dismounted, a couple of men came out carrying a board with a blanket covering it.

'The bank's been robbed,' the blacksmith said, as he followed the men out of the bank.

'Any idea who they were?' Ben shouted over to him as he hitched his horse to the rail.

'Naw,' Bill Dixon, the blacksmith, called back. 'Four strangers. They headed up to Rock Canyon. They took Beth Mason with them.'

Beth Mason was the storekeeper's daughter.

'Start rounding up a posse,' Ben said to Slade. 'Let's get after them.'

They had been riding for an hour, following the tracks up into the canyon, when they found the girl's body.

'It's damn bad,' Ben said when he'd called up the posse to take a look at it.

He watched their faces as he made them walk slowly past the body.

'Why'd you do that?' Slade asked him when they started out again.

'Make sure they know what we're goin' after,

20

them murderin' bastards, and to make sure we catch them. You see the looks on their faces?'

Slade nodded with understanding.

It was getting towards night when they ran the robbers down. The four outlaws had got stuck in a dead-end off-shoot of the main canyon.

'I'm goin' in there an' see if they've got a mind to come out quietly,' Ben told the posse as he got up from the cover of the rocks.

'That's stupid, Ben,' the blacksmith warned him. 'They ain't got anything to lose.'

'I've got to give them the chance to give themselves up,' Ben insisted. He started down to where the outlaws were waiting.

He hadn't gone far when Slade and the rest of them heard him call out, then came a couple of shots. In the dying light they saw Ben go down.

'I'm going down to get Ben,' Slade said, getting up and checking the loads in his gun.

'Just be careful,' Dixon, advised him.

'That's what I aim to do,' Slade said. He moved silently, using the rocks for cover. He had not gone far when he saw Ben's body lying motionless in the dirt.

'We can see you, fella,' a voice called out suddenly. 'An' we're gonna give you what the sheriff got.'

A second later a shot parted the air just above Slade's head.

Ben's body lay out in the open. Slade knew that he didn't have much chance of getting to it without collecting a bullet. He inched his way back to where the posse was waiting for him.

'Couldn't get to him?' Bill asked.

'No,' Slade said shortly. 'It looks like we're gonna have to wait until morning.'

The posse settled down to wait. The blacksmith built a fire. Slade spread the men out across the mouth of the canyon.

'Is this just a dead end?' he asked Dixon when the fella came up with Slade's canteen.

'I think so,' the blacksmith told him. 'I'm like you, I don't know the place too well.'

'Ask somebody who does,' Slade told him.

By now it was full dark, and the last thing he wanted was the outlaws slipping away before anybody knew that they were gone. A few minutes later he heard a shuffling near by and the bulky shape of the blacksmith came up out of the dark.

'There's another way out of here. A narrow trail runs up from the side wall and comes out 'bout a mile away. It's a tight squeeze, but a couple of men can get down there. Should bring us up right behind them,' he said pointing off to the left.

'That's fine,' Slade said. 'Who knows the way?'

'Sam Garth, he knows every trail around here,' the blacksmith told him, spitting out a quid of tobacco.

'Bring him up here,' Slade replied. He watched the blacksmith hurry away.

A few minutes later Dixon returned with a white-bearded old man, whom Slade recalled seeing round town a couple of times.

'Sam Garth,' the man said shoving out his hand.

'OK, Sam, you reckon you can get us up round behind them fellas?' Slade asked him.

Sam hesitated. 'Sure. It ain't no trick. Just get yer men and follow me.'

Slade took the blacksmith, along with Sam, and picked out three men. They moved away from the mouth of the canyon and along a dried-out river bed. The clouds were skittering across the sky as the wind began to blow up strongly. Sam led them a few yards in front of Slade and the others.

'Up this way,' he said after a while, and turned off to his left. The ground started to rise.

After a while Sam stopped them and turned.

'We're higher than they are now,' he whispered.

Slade watched as he pointed to the canyon below.

'I used to come up here looking for gold. There used to be some hereabouts, but I think it all got taken out.'

'Thanks Sam,' Slade told him. 'Wait here until we can see what we're doing, and try to talk sense into them.'

'And if they won't see sense?' Sam asked him.

Slade shrugged. 'It's their choice.'

They settled down to wait, with the wind rising as the night wore on. Gradually, the sky became lighter.

Slade crawled to the edge of the overhang and looked down. It took him a few minutes to pick out the men crouched against the boulders below him. Their horses were tethered to a stunted bush a few yards away. The horses moved restlessly. Picking up a handful of rocks Slade signalled Sam and the others to come up to him. He could hear them crawling through the dust. Sam gazed over the edge. As he did so, Slade tipped the rocks over the edge. At first nothing happened, then one of the outlaws looked up and saw Slade.

'This is it, boys. You gonna come quietly or do we start shooting?' Slade yelled.

The outlaw reacted pretty damn fast. Spinning on to his back, he tossed some lead up at Slade. The lead whined over Slade's head, causing him to jerk himself back out of sight. Sam sent one back. There was a cry of surprise from below.

'You might have got one,' Slade said with a grin.

Sam chuckled as he leaned over the rock to see what was going on down below.

'You bastard,' one of the outlaws screamed, his words being blown around by the wind.

Straight away a piece of lead flew up in Slade's direction.

'We've got them worried,' Slade told Sam as

he peered over the edge and fired at the men below him.

'Then we'd best keep them that way.' Sam laughed as he leaned over the edge and fired down at the outlaws below him.

Slade found himself squinting as the wind rose and howled through the canyon.

'You don't need to worry about them goin' anywhere.' Sam laughed. 'The only way they can get out of here is up the trail a few yards further along.' He pointed with his rifle.

'I just don't want them slipping out of here. This wind could cause us some real trouble,' Slade said.

'There's always that chance,' Sam told him.

'Thanks for that,' Slade said with a grin.

He didn't feel all that confident that he could keep the outlaws where they were, not with it being so dark.

Below them the outlaw, Geoff Keating, and his boys were feeling a heap better. Keating glanced across at Harry Gardner.

'Looks like this wind could be doin' a heap to help us,' he said to his *compadre*.

'Yeah, that's what I was thinking,' Gardner replied, wiping the dust out of his eyes. 'You want me to tell them?' He nodded in the direction of the others.

'No, they'd just slow us down and attract some more lead. Tell them to keep them fellas down the other end of the canyon pinned down. We'll take care of them up there.'

Gardner grinned, revealing his brown, crooked teeth. Keating watched him crawl over to the others.

'I told them,' he said when he had crawled back. 'They seemed happy enough.'

Keating threw a glance in their direction as they faced the posse at the entrance to the canyon. He jerked his head in the direction of the trail. A gust of wind threw up a heap more dust and he and Gardner started to crawl away.

'There's something going on down there,' Sam said, nudging Slade's elbow and pointing downwards.

Slade pulled himself to the edge.

'Where do you suppose them two fellas are off to?' he asked.

'To the trail,' Sam replied, trying to follow the progress of Keating and Gardner, his eyes squinting against the dust and the wind. 'They're getting damn hard to follow in this wind.'

'OK, let's get down there,' Slade said. He got to his feet and moved slowly against the wind.

As they moved away, they heard the sound of gunfire from below them.

'Them boys is getting frisky,' Sam said over his shoulder.

'Yeah, let's just hope our fellas we left down there are a mite friskier,' Slade growled as a gust of wind almost put him on the floor.

The fire from below them intensified. A

couple of times Slade took a look over the edge. Once or twice they heard someone cry out.

'They can't be far away now,' Slade said loudly, shouting to make himself heard over the wind.

The roaring of the wind was making it hard for him to hear anything that Sam was saying. They reached the place where the trails met. Slade hunkered down, his .45 in his hand, cocked and ready. He peered into the swirling dust, trying to make out the two outlaws as they came up the trail. Then a hunk of lead whipped past his head, ricocheting off the rock in front of him. The shards of rock just missed his eyes. Slade spun round, aware of Sam reeling back, holding his face. Keating came into sight. Slade fired. The gun bucked and spat out flame and death. Keating's hand went to his throat, the scarlet blood spurting through his fingers, his eyes rolling upwards.

Slade turned to see Gardner cocking his gun and getting ready to fire. He rolled away. Gardner's shot ploughed into the dirt as Slade's own bullet ripped into his heart. Gardner staggered backwards, his knees buckling as he went down.

For a moment Slade lay in the dust, then he remembered Sam. He got up, holstered his gun and went back to where Sam lay. It didn't need a doctor to tell him that Sam was dead. The hole between his eyes told him that.

He tried to get to his feet, but the wind held

him for a second, then he pushed himself up and started down the trail. He had thought about going back and getting a couple of the men from the posse, but decided against it. With the wind and the dust blowing about, they would probably wind up shooting at each other. He had to get Sam's body and check that the other outlaws were dead.

He moved from one boulder to another, using them as shelter from the wind and as cover from the remaining outlaws should they decide to come up.

Larkin and Midgely, the two remaining outlaws, were finding the going tougher than they had thought it might be. Larkin had taken a flesh wound and Midgely had had his scalp grazed. His hat lay ten feet away where a bullet had dropped it. He had sworn loudly when this had happened and had sent a flurry of shots towards the posse.

'That posse's gonna get lucky sooner or later,' he shouted to Larkin.

'Yeah, I was thinking that,' Larkin called over to him.

Larkin turned to try and see the others, but he could see no sign of them.

'Where do you suppose them two have gone?'

Midgley strained his eyes to see through the dust.

'One thing's fer sure, they ain't here,' he shouted, with a macabre laugh.

'Them two bastards have run out on us,' Larkin yelled.

'We'd better get out as well,' Midgely shouted back as he pushed fresh loads into his gun.

They both got to their feet and moved slowly towards the trail, sending the occasional hunk of lead in the direction of the posse.

'OK, we ain't stayin' here on our own,' Midgely called to Larkin as he tossed another shot down at a member of the posse who had shown himself.

He heard the man yell and fall, clutching his belly.

'I reckon now's the time,' Midgely hollered as he got up from the cover of the rocks.

'OK,' Larkin called back and jumped to his feet.

Through the dust he could see Midgely coming his way.

They grabbed the leathers of their horses and led them out.

'Don't just sit there,' Midgely yelled as he went past him.

Midgely turned and rode after him, his horse pulling at the leathers, the wind and dust blinding him. He stuck his gun in his holster and followed. They rode between the rocks. Slade saw them but it was too late as they disappeared into the dust. He turned to fire, but there were a couple of his boys in there somewhere. Slade moved forward in the direction that Midgely and

Larkin had taken. There was no sign of them. He listened carefully, but all he could hear was the wind.

Midgely and Larkin rode on.

'That you, Deputy?' a voice shouted out behind Slade as the wind whipped it away.

'Yeah, it's me,' Slade called out, his hand cupped to his mouth.

'Lost them, huh?' the undertaker asked, sliding his gun into its holster.

'Yeah, you could say that.' Slade blinked against the dust storm.

'I was looking forward to seeing them boys dangle after what they did back there,' the undertaker said, jerking his thumb to where they had found the girl's body.

'I'm goin' after them,' Slade shouted over the wind.

The undertaker wiped the dust out of his eyes and squinted hard as the wind blew the dust back again.

'You want me an' some of the boys to come with you?' he asked Slade.

Slade thought about it for a minute, then said, 'No, you've got wives and families back there and them two are damn dangerous.'

A feeling of relief came over the undertaker. At least he'd made the offer.

They went to where the rest of the posse were waiting and Slade told them what had happened. With the wind still raising the dust and the devil, he rode out after them.

Midgely and Larkin were looking over their shoulders, trying to see if anybody was following them as they rowelled their horses and headed off down the trail.

Somewhere behind them Slade was climbing into the saddle and going off in the direction they had gone in. He didn't have much hope of finding them right off. He put his bandanna over his mouth and rode with his head down. The wind was pulling at his clothes, and only the leather thong under his chin stopped his hat being pulled off his head.

THREE

Ahead of him Larkin and Midgely had come down the other side of the mountain, and were starting to feel that they might be in the clear. Larkin pulled up close to Midgely, and leaned over in his saddle, holding on to his hat.

'We're gonna have to keep going for a spell,' he shouted over the howling wind.

They rode on until they came to some abandoned buildings. Larkin got down and looked round.

'Seems like an old stage-station. We can rest up here for a while. Give this storm a chance to blow itself out. Can't see anybody following us in this.'

'Might be you're right,' Midgely shouted over to him.

The bars of the fence had been broken down and the bars smashed. Up ahead they saw the old building with its doors banging in the wind. Most of the windows had been smashed. Larkin dismounted and tethered his horse to the remains of the hitch rail. Midgely followed suit.

'We'll just take a look inside, then put the horses in the stable round the back, if it's still standing,' Larkin said, drawing his sixgun and looking round.

As they went in, the sound of the wind died away as did its force.

'There ain't nobody here,' Midgely said, putting his gun away. He suddenly found himself shouting in the silence.

'Git a fire going. There's some wood in the box over there,' Larkin told him, pointing to the corner. 'I'll get the horses stabled down.'

'Spooky, ain't it?' Midgely said.

'You scared or somethin'?' Larkin asked with contempt in his voice.

Midgely did as he was told and started to gather the wood for the fire and heap it into the pot-bellied stove. Outside, Larkin untied the horses and led them round to the back. The stable was still standing, just about, but there were a couple of holes in the roof. Looking up at them, he spat, and tethered the horses in the most sheltered place he could find. He took off their saddles, and settled them down.

'I've got the fire goin',' Midgely said to him.

Larkin watched the flames dancing on the wall. He tossed Midgely a can of beans and a hunk of stale bread and some bacon that he had brought in with him.

'Do what you can do with them,' he said.

Midgely caught them and searched round for something to cook them in.

'I'm gonna take a look round. Don't want any nasty surprises.' Larkin checked the loads in his gun and went outside.

Slade had lost the trail and was thinking about turning round to get to the posse again, but he decided to give it a while longer. The wind had slackened and he could see some more as the dust wasn't flying about so much. Pulling down the bandanna, he got his canteen from the saddle horn and swilled his mouth out with the water. He spat it on to the ground, put the canteen on his saddle horn again, and looked around him.

With the slackening of the wind, he could see a lot further. A low range of hills stood off to his left. Rowelling his horse he headed for the hills and urged his horse on up the shallow slope. At the top he could see the old stage-station.

Pulling his horse's head round he headed down the slope in the direction of the station. By the time he'd got to the flat ground the wind had dropped altogether and the air was becoming warm and still again. Slade dismounted half a mile from the station and threaded his way between the rocks. He could see no sign of any occupants of the station, then he saw the faintest wisp of smoke being tossed about as it went up into the lightening sky.

At the gate he stopped and had another look round. He could still see no one. He ran in through the gate, using a broken-down wagon as cover. Slade cat-footed round the wagon. For a moment he hesitated, then moved across towards the window. Inside he could make out Midgely fixing up some food. Midgely had his back to the door and was struggling to open the tin that Larkin had tossed him.

'Takin' a keen interest in something that ain't any of yer business.' The voice of Larkin took him by surprise. 'Drop the gun.'

Slade opened his hand and let the gun fall to the ground.

'Git inside,' Larkin ordered him.

Midgely didn't hear the door open as Larkin pushed Slade inside.

'Soon be eatin',' he said without turning round.

'Just make sure there's enough for our unexpected guest,' Larkin snapped.

Midgely turned quickly, dropping the can to the floor as he saw Slade and the star on his chest.

'Who the hell's this fella?' he demanded angrily.

'By the star on his vest, I'd say he was the deputy from that town we've bin through,' Larkin said with a laugh.

'What are we gonna do with him?' Midgely asked.

'We can make start by tying him up,' Larkin snarled. 'Get a rope from somewhere.'

Midgely had a look round before he saw one in the corner by the stove.

Larkin watched him while he cut a length off.

'Now git him tied up. And you don't try anything slick or you'll get a bullet,' Larkin said, waggling his gun under Slade's nose.

Midgely grabbed Slade's arms and forced them up his back. The rope bit into Slade's flesh, causing him to wince.

'Over in that corner,' Larkin said, giving him a push to get him going.

Slade staggered into the corner, and fell in a heap.

'What are we gonna do with him?' Midgely asked Larkin as he stirred the beans into a dirty pan that he had found.

'Can't you guess what we're gonna have to do with him?' Larkin bawled at Midgely.

'You mean we're gonna have to kill him, like we did to that girl?' Midgely asked nervously.

'Guess so, unless he decides to do it himself, which he ain't likely to do,' Larkin went on.

Midgely turned white.

'I didn't hold with what you did to that girl,' he said, giving Slade a look.

'Well it's done now,' Larkin said cutting off a

hunk of bacon and tossing it to Midgely. 'And we'll all hang together if them other two fellas get out of that jam we left them in, which I don't think they will.'

Midgely turned back to the pot and gave it a another stir. He picked up the bacon and started it cooking.

All the time Slade watched them and said nothing.

Once or twice he pulled at the ropes and found some give in them. They were old ropes and he didn't figure it would take much to get them to part. It was just a question of waiting. The two outlaws fixed up their meal and got down to eating it, taking no notice of Slade.

As they ate Slade pulled at the ropes and felt them beginning to part. Larkin took out a bottle and took a long drink from it, then handed it to Midgely, who took a mouthful and passed it back.

'You soon had your fill,' Larkin told him and put the bottle to his lips.

Larkin offered it to Midgely who waved it away.

'Suit yourself,' Larkin said morosely and took another long drink from the bottle.

As the level of the whiskey went down Slade pulled at the rope, and parted it.

When the bottle was empty, Larkin's head fell forward on to his arms.

Slade recollected that his gun was still outside

on the veranda, and although Midgely was frightened and nervous Slade knew better than to go up against him without a gun.

Midgely reached for the coffee-pot.

'Got enough in there for me?' Slade asked him.

Surprised, Midgely looked round.

'Yeah, I guess,' he said, picking up the pot and getting up from the chair.

Tensing himself Slade watched as he came over, holding the pot in front of him.

Judging him to be within distance, Slade sprang at him, knocking the pot from his hand. The coffee spilled all over Midgely's hands, causing him to scream in pain.

Larkin's head stirred at the scream. Slade's balled fist landed in Midgely's belly, doubling him up. Larkin stirred again. Midgely cannoned into him. Slade grabbed the pistol from his holster.

'Wake him up,' he yelled at Midgely.

Midgely scrambled across the table, grabbed Larkin by the shoulder and began to shake him violently.

'Come on,' he yelled, throwing a nervous glance at Slade, who was holding the gun on him, his hand not wavering.

'Huh – what's goin' on?' Larkin asked, raising his head from the table.

'This is what's going on,' Slade yelled at him as he fired a shot into the air.

Larkin's head came up real sharp when he heard the shot.

'Now sit still,' Slade ordered him, pointing the gun at his heart.

For a moment Larkin stared dumbly at him.

'You stupid bastard,' he screamed at Midgely. 'How'd you let him get loose?'

'Damnit, you tied the ropes,' Midgely yelled, as his hand started to swell up.

'It wasn't hard,' Slade told him. 'Now, you go and get that rope off my saddle horn, and be quick about it.' Slade snapped.

Midgely ran for the door and went outside. When he came back, Slade had got Larkin to straddle a chair.

'Get him tied up, and then fry me up some of that bacon you've got left there.'

He watched as Midgely tied Larkin up. When he had finished he tested the ropes.

'They're fine,' he said. 'Now get to fixing that bacon.'

While Midgely was cooking the bacon, Slade ran his hands over Larkin's body after he had taken the sixgun out of its holster. He found a long knife in Larkin's boot. He took it out and put it into his own belt.

'How come you got mixed up with scum like this?' Slade asked, cutting up a piece of the bacon and forking it into his mouth.

'It's a long story,' Midgely began miserably.

'We've got plenty of time,' Slade told him,

pouring himself a fresh cup of coffee.

For a minute Midgely thought and then shook his head.

'I can't rightly say.' He spoke slowly.

'You'd better start thinking,' Slade replied, watching the narrow face. 'They're gonna be hanging you when we get back. You and him.'

Midgely paled as Slade spoke.

'You're frightening the boy to death.' The figure in the chair laughed.

'Keep quiet,' Slade ordered him over his shoulder.

'There ain't nothing you can do,' Larkin went on. 'He knows he's gonna hang. Unless he gets me out of this chair and gives me a gun.'

Midgely glanced across to him, like maybe he was thinking about it.

'We'll get out of here in about an hour or so,' Slade said, finishing the food on his plate.

He went to the door and looked up at the grey sky. By now it was as light as it was going to get. They lapsed into silence, with Larkin giving the other two some hard looks.

'I'm going to tie you up while I go out and check them horses, and get mine from over yonder,' Slade told Midgely. He cut a piece of rope, and tied Midgely's hands behind him.

'We're gonna have to think of somethin' damn quick,' Larkin hissed to Midgely when Slade had gone out. 'They're gonna hang us like he said, an' it don't matter that you didn't go along with what we did to that girl, you're still gonna hang.'

The bile welled up in Midgely's throat as he felt the rope tighten round his neck and the trapdoor open beneath his feet.

He hadn't wanted to get tied up with Larkin and the rest of them, but it just seemed to happen. Maybe if things had turned out different, like his kid sister not needing money for medicine, and his pa being able to hold down a steady job instead of spending his time in the saloon. Then he wouldn't have had to go looking for work. When he couldn't find work, if somebody had been around to stop him from taking up with the low life of the town, and maybe if he hadn't been wearing a gun and hadn't accidentally shot the sheriff, he might have been all right, but things hadn't turned out that way, and now he was looking at a rope.

Larkin twisted on the bunk when he heard Slade coming along the boardwalk.

'You gonna help me or him?' Larkin asked Midgely.

'I'm getting a better break than you gave me,' Midgely said.

'Then I'll see you in hell,' Larkin snarled at him.

The door opened and Slade came in. He looked at them both.

'What's been going on? he asked them.

Larkin turned to face the wall. Midgely said nothing.

'All right,' he said to Midgely. 'I guess I'm gonna have to tighten the ropes. I figured I could trust you.'

He pulled the ropes tighter around Midgely's hands.

'I'm going to get some fresh water in the canteens from the stream, then we can get out of here.'

Outside, he took the canteens from the saddles and walked down to the stream and filled them. When he came back neither man had moved.

'Time to be going, boys,' he said, hauling Larkin off the bunk and pushing him to the door. He did the same with Midgely.

FOUR

Outside, he helped them into the saddle and rode out with them. They had ridden for a spell in silence when Slade heard shooting up ahead. Getting up ahead of the two prisoners, he grabbed the leathers and hauled the horses off the trail into some cover.

'Keep quiet until I can see what's going on,' he told them.

Slade rode back to the edge of the covering and listened. The shooting was getting closer. Slade drew his .45, and waited. A few moments later a horseman came round the bend, tossing lead over his shoulder. He galloped past where Slade was hiding; as he did so a couple of masked men came by, firing at him, their horses throwing up dust and rocks as they came.

Just as they passed by him, Slade rode out of the cover and went after them, rowelling his horse, and tossing lead after them. One of the masked men fell from the saddle, grasping at his back. A second shot from Slade took the hat off the other man, causing him to haul quickly on the leathers of his horse, throw down his gun and put his hands into the air.

'All right, all right,' he shouted. 'I've had enough.'

'Glad you see it that way,' Slade told him.

Keeping the robber covered, he looked down the trail to see if he could see anything of the victim. After a minute or so, a figure appeared from up the trail holding his gun and looking cautious.

'It's OK, I'm the law,' Slade shouted to him.

'I'm sure glad to see you,' the rider said, sliding the gun back into the leather. 'My horse is plain tuckered out and these fellas were just beginning to catch up with me.'

'I'm taking a couple of prisoners back,' Slade said slowly, suddenly remembering Larkin and Midgely. 'Keep an eye on this fella while I go and see if my prisoners are still safe and sound.'

Slade galloped away, and found Larkin and Midgley where he had left them.

'Let's get going,' he said to them, leading the horses on to the trail.

'I'm Brent Travers,' the rider said to Slade when he got the prisoners back to him. 'I was riding to Red Rim with some payroll money for the Big S ranch.'

'You were damn lucky I was out this way,' Slade told him, as he tied up the prisoner.

'I know him,' Travers said.

'Not a friend of yours.' Slade smiled.

'Hell, no. He used to work on the Big S. Goes by the name of Gary Smiley. That's his *amigo* over there, Harry Gallagher. Got fired a while ago for running off some of the boss's cattle, and selling them to another rancher.'

'So they figured they'd get even by helping themselves to some of his cash?' Slade said to Travers.

'Damn right they did,' Travers said. 'I thought I saw them following me round town last week. So, I guess they were picking their moment.'

'Well, they picked it for the last time. Especially him.' Slade nodded to the corpse by the side of the trail.

They slung Gallagher's body over the saddle and rode on. Travers was the ramrod of the Big S outfit until he'd taken a bad fall which limited him pretty much as to what he could do. So they'd kept him on, doing any work he could around the spread.

It didn't take them long to get back to town. The rest of the posse had made it back. Things were pretty quiet when everybody found out that Ben had been killed.

It seemed to Slade that his first job would be to stop the folks in town from lynching the two men he had brought in.

'Shame about Ben,' Jake Smith, leader of the town council, said to Slade when he told him what had happened.

For a while Jake said nothing, just contemplating the end of his cigar.

'You're a mite young for this job,' he said, biting off the end. 'But there's nobody else round here interested in the job. What about you?'

'I guess so,' Slade told him straight away. He had been thinking about it on the way in with his prisoners. 'That's if the rest of the council agree.'

'They will,' Smith said, lighting his cigar.

When Smith had gone out Slade sat in the chair behind the desk. The three prisoners had been locked up. Smith came back to the office half an hour later looking pleased with himself.

'I've been round the council and they're all in favour, but a couple of them think yer a bit young, and you ain't had Ben's experience. I just hope you do as good a job as Ben,' Smith said, rooting for a match to light his cigar with.

'I'll do my best,' Slade told him, with less confidence than he felt.

'I'm sure you'll do all right,' Smith replied, lighting his cigar.

When he had gone out Slade checked the prisoners, and went back to the front office. The night was starting to fall when the door opened. At first Slade did not recognize the woman.

'I just came to thank you again,' she began.

'Thank me?' Slade asked, leaning forward on

the desk.

'Sure, fer stopping that fella taking my earnings.'

Then Slade recognized her as the whore he had saved from getting robbed in he alley.

'My name's Millie, remember?' she told him.

He felt himself colour up as she came into the office and sat on the edge of his desk, her skirt riding up over her long legs. Slade had never had much to do with women, apart from now. The smell of her perfume and her looks made him feel strange in a way that he had never felt since the last time that Millie had thanked him.

'I've got a room over Black Bob's saloon. I could show you how grateful I was again. From what the mayor was telling me, you did a good job in bringin' in them fellas that did for the girl.' Millie moved quickly to stop the strap of her dress from falling off her shoulder.

'I'm not sure if I'll be able to do that,' Slade said, shifting uneasily in his chair. 'I ain't got no deputy, an' I figure it would be wrong to go missing on my first night at work, especially with them prisoners to guard.'

'You don't worry about that. I'll get Jake to keep an eye on things while I'm entertaining you. He owes me a favour. He wouldn't want his wife to find out where he spends a couple of hours on Friday nights,' she said with a knowing grin. 'You come across about ten. It's room eight,' she said getting up to leave.

'All right, if you're sure it'll be all right,' Slade said thinking how hot it had become in the office all of a sudden.

The night was quiet, and Slade found himself watching the clock. At a quarter to eleven Smith walked in.

'You just go along and collect yer reward. Just don't be all night.' He took a shotgun from the rack, and broke it open, Slade handed him a couple of shells.

Slade walked down to the saloon. Black Bob Dyer saw him coming in through the batwing doors and waved him up the stairs. It was louder upstairs than he'd realized when he was coming into the saloon. There was plenty of noise coming from the rooms on either side of the whore's.

Slade knocked on the door and waited.

'Come in,' Millie called out.

Slade let himself in. Millie was standing facing the window looking out across the street.

'Glad Jake decided to give you some time off,' she said, turning from the window with a wry smile on her face.

The gown she was wearing was thin and blue and transparent, and made Slade feel real uncomfortable.

'Come over here and sit down,' Millie said, patting the bed.

Slade went over and sat down. The whore moved away from the window and opened a bottle on the table. Then she filled two glasses and handed one to Slade.

'You're shaking,' she said with a grin as she sat down on the bed next to him.

'I feel shaky,' Slade said as some of the champagne spilled over the edge of the glass.

'Here, I'll take it,' she said, folding her hand round the glass.

A feeling of excitement ran through Slade as she eased the glass out of his hand.

Reaching out to the table she put the glass down, then peeled off her robe, thrusting out her breasts as she did so.

'Enjoying the view?' she asked in a quiet husky voice, running her hands over her white flesh.

'You could say that,' he answered, his voice thick with lust.

When it was over, Slade lay back, warm and contented.

The whore filled out a couple more glasses of the champagne.

'How are you feeling?' she asked him.

'It's kinda hard to say,' he replied. 'Sorta great.'

The whore laughed. 'I aim to please. That's you and the boss paid off.'

'I'd forgotten about him,' Slade said, suddenly trying to get up from the bed.

The whore put her hand in the middle of his chest, and pushed him back.

'You've got a bonus comin', while it was yer first time,' she laughed.

*

Jake was sitting in the sheriff's chair when Slade got to the office. His eyes opened suddenly and his hand reached for the shotgun.

'Take it easy,' Slade told him as he closed the door behind himself.

'Your prisoners have been keeping pretty quiet,' Jake said, getting up and stretching.

'Glad to hear it,' Slade said.

'You'd best hope things keep quiet,' Jake went on.

'Why's that?' Slade asked in an uneasy tone of voice.

'Ben was mighty damn popular round here, and I've heard some talk that some people might want to hang these fellas before a jury says they should hang.'

It took a couple of seconds for it to sink in. Then Slade realized what Jake was saying.

'They're gonna try and lynch them?' he asked.

'Nothing more certain from the way I heard it,' Jake said.

'Can I count on any help?' Slade picked up the shotgun and checked the loads.

' 'Fraid not,' Jake replied. 'Ben was mighty popular. A lot of people are gonna come lookin' for these fellas.' Jake went out.

When he had gone Slade sat down and gazed at the desk. It was damned strange, he thought to himself. He'd spent all that time and effort along with the posse in getting the killers back, now he was going to have to make sure many of the same people didn't lynch them.

He picked up the shotgun again and broke it open. As he did so he heard a sound outside. A mob was heading his way. Slade went to the window and looked out.

It was like the night they had come for his pa, but this time there would be somebody in the jail ready to defend the prisoners whether they were guilty or not. He went to the door, opened it and went and stood on the veranda, his shotgun held high across his chest. The crowd was getting closer and most of them were wearing hoods.

Raising the shot gun, Slade fired a round into the night air. For a moment the crowd stopped.

'Just hand them over, Sheriff.' A voice came from the rear of the mob. 'We know what to do with them.'

'And I know what to do with this,' Slade answered as loudly as he could.

'Quit stallin' Sheriff,' the same voice said. 'We just want them for what they did to Ben and the girl.'

The crowd was moving forward again. Slade knew that he had just one barrel left and five loads in his .45. His hand was sweating as he tightened his grip round the butt of the gun. He knew the mess a shotgun would make at close range, and he didn't want to use it, but he was the sheriff and what had happened to his pa came back to him. The last thing he wanted to do was to fire into the mob. The mob had started to spread out forming a semicircle around him. Time was getting short.

'I know most of you.' He was aware that his mouth was dry and his voice hoarse, and that he was frightened, but they weren't taking prisoners like his pa had been taken out and strung up to a tree like some kind of animal.

'Your last warning,' he said, hefting the gun.

The mob wavered and stopped again. None of them moved.

'Come on, Sheriff,' the same voice from the back called out. 'Hand them over. We ain't no quarrel with you.'

'If you want them, you come and get them. Just you.' Slade took a step off the veranda and walked determinedly towards the crowd.

The nearer he got to them, the more he sensed their irresolution. The distance between them and himself became less and less. Once he got within arm's reach they started to draw away from him, leaving a passage for him to get to the hooded figure at the back. At last they were face to face. The crowd melted away from him. A surge of confidence ran through Slade.

'Let's see who's hiding behind that mask,' he shouted so that everybody could hear him.

The figure beneath the hood winced as Slade

reached out and grabbed it. He jerked it off.

'Haven't you seen enough killing?' he demanded of the dead girl's father.

The man winced and lowered his head. Nobody moved.

'I'm taking you to jail,' Slade shouted so that everybody could hear him.

Lowering the shotgun, he grabbed the man by the shirt-front, and pushed him out in front of the crowd. The man reeled and fell to the ground. Slade jerked him up and led him to the jail. Behind him, the crowd started to drift silently away, just as they had done when his pa had been lynched.

The other prisoners were at the bars of their cells when Slade took the new prisoner down there.

'I didn't do this for you,' he told them angrily when they started to thank him.

The rest of the night was pretty quiet. Slade felt fairly pleased with himself when Jake came by the following morning.

'Heard you did a good job last night,' Jake said. 'It's the kind of thing Ben would have done. Yeah, we're all damn proud of you.'

'Glad you think so,' Slade replied wishing he could get out for some breakfast.

'Yeah, looks like we made the right choice.' Jake smiled in a self-satisfied way.

When he had left Jake to watch the prisoners Slade went down to the eats place. People were looking at him differently, he realized, as he went down there. Slade had found some self-respect, and he felt different somehow. It was only when he sat down to the full plate of food that he knew that he had grown up a lot in the last couple of months. Looking at it now, he realized that he was a different person, that the young Jack Slade was gone for good. The new one might take some living with.

The week ended and another week began then a month and before he knew it he had been sheriff for a year. Very occasionally did he get nightmares about the night his pa had been lynched. Larkin and Midgley were hanged, so was the fella who had tried to rob the hand from the Big S. Slade found himself getting into a routine. It wore at his nerves. Nothing much seemed to happen in his town. A lot of people put it down to the kind of sheriff they had, but it still irked Slade and he started to feel restless. Maybe it was time to move on. He had visions of himself growing old as the sheriff or maybe not living long enough to grow old. Maybe he would wind up lying in the street with a bullet in him. He made up his mind.

It was Millie who was the most tearful when he told her. Slade had been going over occasionally, and had come to like the girl.

'Shucks, Slade,' she said between the tears. 'I'm gonna miss you. You were a damn nice fella

to have around. I'm sure gonna miss you.'
   'I'm gonna miss you too,' he told her.

FIVE

The next day Slade rode out, and for some reason he wasn't sorry. He headed south with no clear idea of where he was going or what he was going to do when he got there.

It was a few days before Slade came to a town. He hauled up outside a saloon, tethered his horse to the hitch rail and went inside. The night had started to close in and the place was full and noisy. Half a dozen girls were doing a high-stepping dance on the stage at the back of the place with three men grinding out a tune for them, to the hurrahs and cheers of the customers.

Slade pushed his way to the bar and ordered a beer. It took the barkeep a while to serve him with all the other customers he had.

'Sorry about that bud,' he said when he had taken Slade's order.

'It's OK,' Slade told him laying down the coins for the beer and looking round the place.

'Lot of commotion in here tonight,' he said to the barkeep. 'Seems like something pretty exciting's happening.'

'New singer come in on the stage from back East. As well as being downright pretty, she can sing as well.'

'That's always an advantage,' Slade said, who had known singers who could neither sing and were downright ugly as well.

'You can say that agin,' the barkeep said, wiping the bar top. He went to serve another customer.

Slade turned to watch the dancing girls cavorting round the stage. Suddenly the girls danced to the centre of the stage, let out a whoop, and did the splits, their heads bent touching the floor of the stage.

A couple of guns went off and everybody in the place was yelling and shouting. A fella in a smart tuxedo came on to the stage, and called for order. The crowd quietened down considerably as he spoke to announce the singer.

'Miss Grace Everard, straight from New Orleans,' he announced, flinging his arms up in an extravagant manner.

Once again the crowd erupted as a slim red-haired girl came out on to the stage.

Slade put his glass down with a start when he saw her. The barkeep had been right. She was pretty. Bracing himself Slade waited to hear if she could sing. Again, the barkeep was right. She could sing. Slade listened, his beer forgotten. When the song finished, the crowd demanded another and Miss Grace Everard obliged. When that was finished they demanded another, and so on until she had sung five.

'No more, gentlemen. I am quite exhausted,' she said, in a Southern accent.

The crowd weren't about to take that as the end of her act, and things started looking ugly. Somebody fired a shot into the air.

'If you insist, gentlemen,' Grace Everard said breathlessly, signalling to the men below her.

'We do,' the crowd roared at her.

'But definitely the last.'

The redhead bowed gracefully and started to sing again. When she had finished the crowd erupted once more. There was more shooting and even more yelling than last time.

'That's it gentlemen,' Grace Everard said, holding her hands to her breast and breathing hard as she did so.

From the way she was talking, and moving off the stage, the crowd knew it was the end. With a quick curtsy, she turned and disappeared from the stage.

Turning to his beer, Slade picked it up and signalled for another. As he did so there was the sound of men bursting into the saloon.

'The bank's bin robbed,' one of them yelled.

'What do you mean?' a harsh voice asked from the end of the bar nearest the door.

'I mean the bank's been robbed, Ray,' the man yelled again.

Ray Holland, the sheriff, stepped away from the crowd, and headed for the batwing doors. The crowd started to follow him.

Slade stayed where he was.

'Much money in the bank?' he asked the barkeep when the place was empty.

'Plenty. Can't remember the last time we had a robbery in this town.'

They chewed the fat for a while.

'You got a room for the night?' Slade asked the barkeep.

'Sure,' the barkeep said, taking a key from under the counter. 'Just up the stairs. Number five, right next to Grace Everard's manager.'

Slade took the key and went up the stairs. At the top he saw Grace Everard talking to a fella he took to be her manager. As soon as they saw him coming they stopped talking. Grace Everard gave Slade an appraising glance as he went past. Slade unlocked the room door and went inside. The first thing he did was light a lamp, and sit on the edge of the bed. A few minutes later, he heard Grace Everard's manager's room door close.

Slade got out of his trousers and shirt, filled up a bowl of water, and cleaned himself up. The bedclothes were cool and fresh after his long ride. It took him about ten seconds to get to sleep.

It was still dark when he woke up. At first he didn't know what it was that had woken him. Then he realized that it was voices coming from the room next door. Slade rolled on to his back and pushed the blankets clear of his body. The voices weren't loud but they were low and persistent and heated.

By now he was wide awake and starting to feel resentful at being woken up. He couldn't make out what they were arguing about, but it must be important, he told himself. He knew the woman's voice was Grace Everard's, and guessed that the other voice belonged to her manager. Slade figured they were arguing about the money they had got for Grace Everard's performance. The words 'money' and 'takings' kept coming up. Grace Everard was complaining about not getting her fair share of the money. Rolling over on to his side he tried to get back to sleep. The next thing he knew the sun was shining through the window. Still half-asleep he struggled out of bed, and rinsed his face off.

The barkeep from last night was sweeping the place out.

'Don't happen to serve breakfast do you?' he asked the fella.

The barkeep stopped sweeping and leaned on his brush.

'You just go through the door,' he said, indicating a door at the far end of the bar. 'I'll be with you in a minute.'

'What happened at the bank last night?' Slade asked him.

'Bank got cleaned out. Only thing that was left was a couple of bills. Everything just went, along with the silver and all the gold they had in there.'

When Slade had eaten he went down to the livery stable to get his horse. On the way out of town he passed the posse coming home. He didn't have to be told they hadn't had any luck. He had been on a few posses like that himself.

After a while, as he was moving down a narrow canyon, he heard shooting up ahead of him. Rowelling his horse, he drew his sixgun. As he came out of the canyon, he saw a buggy standing in the middle of the trail, up to its axle in soft sand. Beside it he saw Grace Everard, and her manager cowering from the gunfire. The fella was making some pretty lame efforts to send some lead into the stand of trees by the trail. When he reached the buggy, Slade jumped out of the saddle and began to fire in the direction of the trees, figuring a robbery was going on.

He could see that Grace Everard was holding the side of her head. A line of blood ran down her face. She looked terrified. Taking a line on the trees, Slade sent up a couple of hunks of lead. He heard a shout of pain, and saw someone fall from behind the trees. He was about to send up another piece of lead when he heard a grunt of pain and Grace Everard's manager slumped to the ground, holding his chest. Slade reached down, but could see that it was no good.

A couple more bullets slammed into the buggy. The horses skittered nervously, and pulled at the buggy. A figure showed himself long enough for Slade to put a piece of lead into him. He toppled to the ground. There was a halt in the firing, and a couple of minutes later Slade heard horses galloping away.

He turned to see Grace Everard weeping quietly, her body shaking. Cautiously, Slade cat-footed to where the outlaws had been firing from. Behind the trees he saw a mess of tracks leading up the tree-covered slope.

At the buggy, Grace Everard was still weeping silently. Slade tried a couple of times to get some sense out of her, but couldn't get anywhere.

'You're gonna have to pull yourself together,' he said to her, trying to get her to stand up.

He tried a couple more times, but she just sat on the buggy weeping.

Slade took a look round. 'I'm gonna have to take you back to town,' he said to her. It took Slade the better part of an hour to dig the buggy out with his bare hands, then he hitched his own horse to it. The three horses strained at the leathers and eventually with a jerk the buggy was free.

The bags in the buggy had come loose from their straps. As he picked them up to fix them, Slade noticed that a brown bag had come open.

As he closed it, he saw the greenbacks inside, along with some gold coins. The greenbacks had a band round them which gave the name of the town bank. He fingered them and realized that they were the takings from the bank. Beside him Grace Everard was still crying quietly.

'Seems like you have got some slick talking to do when we get back to town,' he said to her.

There was no reply, just the steady sound of her sobbing. Slade tied his horse to the front of the buggy, and flicked the leathers across the other horses' backs. The buggy jolted and set off in the direction of town.

Ray Holland was sitting at his desk in the office, a half-drunk mug of coffee in front of him, a weary look on his face, when Slade walked in hauling Grace Everard behind him. She was still sobbing in a muffled way.

Holland looked up suddenly when Slade slammed the door shut.

'What in hell's name's this?' he asked when Slade pulled a heap of bills out of the bag and dropped them on the table.

As Slade told the sheriff what had happened the sheriff's face became angrier and angrier.

'This town made you welcome,' he snapped at Grace Everard. 'And this is the thanks they get for it.' He looked at Slade. 'I'm gonna lock her up. You wait here.'

When he had gone out, Slade settled himself

in the chair opposite Holland's, and waited for the lawman to come back.

'Thanks fer bringing her in. I'll get the posse together again and get them bodies that you left out there,' Holland said, handing over the makings to Slade.

'Thanks.' Slade started to build a stogie. As he did so a thought struck him.

'This Grace Everard and her manager, I expect they've been in the territory singing in other places?'

For a moment Holland didn't see the point, then his stubbly face lit up.

'I'll get down to the telegraph office, and wire some of the other towns hereabouts, see if they've had the same thing happening to them.'

'I'll walk down there with you,' Slade said, stubbing out the remains of the stogie.

'Whatever you say,' Holland said. He got up from the desk.

A couple of hours later they had their answer. Three towns where Grace Everard had played had been hit on the night that she sang there.

'As far as I'm concerned that's it,' Holland said as they sat in his office drinking coffee and reading the answers to the telegrams. 'I'll take a posse out to where the shooting was, and see if we can pick up the trail from there. You coming along as well?'

'Sure,' Slade said getting up from the chair.

It didn't take Holland long to get the posse together.

'Sure, that's him,' Holland said when he stood over the manager's body.

'Got two more up here, Ray,' his deputy called down from the trees.

Slade and Holland walked up to where the deputy was hunkering down over the body of one of the men Slade had shot.

'Can't say I know him,' Holland said, when he saw the man's face.

'Nor me,' Slade said.

'You boys go up the trail, see what you can pick up,' Holland ordered the posse.

The deputy came back a few minutes later.

'We've found this, Ray,' the deputy said, pointing to a trail of blood that ran up the slope.

'Let's follow it and see where it takes us,' the sheriff said.

The posse followed him down the slope and around and down the other side where a lazy river flowed quietly by. A jetty ran out into the water. Some boats were tied there, and a rope trailed into the water.

'This rope's been cut recently,' Slade said, holding up a frayed end.

'Didn't think anybody still used this place,' Ray said to him as he examined the rope. 'Trappers used to bring their catches up here, then take them down into town. Never heard of anybody using it for a spell though.'

'Frank, you take them horses downriver. Me and Slade and the rest of the boys will come down in the other boats.'

'OK, Ray,' Frank called out. He holstered his gun and led a few of the boys off with the horses.

'Only trouble with this is that when it gets downstream a few miles, there's some rapids that can be mighty rough,' Ray said to Slade as he got into the boat behind and picked up an oar.

The first couple of miles were pretty calm, like Ray had said, then Slade noticed the water getting white as it fetched up against the grey rocks. The boats became harder and harder to handle, and it took the oarsmen all their time to keep them from being swept against the rocks. The river fell into a black gorge, flanked by sheer walls of rock. On top of the rocks, Slade could see pine trees.

'How much further is there to go?' Slade shouted above the increased roaring of the water.

'More than I remember,' Ray gasped out between deep lungfuls of air. The water was getting rougher with each yard. Black rocks suddenly sprouted from beneath the surface like jagged teeth. Slade watched as one of the boats smashed into one and was torn to pieces, its crew flung into the water. One by one the three men were sucked out of sight, screaming as they went under.

'That's the way we're gonna go if we ain't careful,' a frightened voice behind Slade said.

'Then we'd better keep our minds on what we're doing,' Slade called out over the roar of the water.

A wave slammed against the side of the boat, driving it towards the shore. Slade and the others struggled to keep the oars from being torn out of their hands. The handle of the oar tore the skin of his left hand, and he felt the warm blood surge over his flesh. The pain burned into him and he let out a cry. Behind him, he could hear the others gasping and struggling to keep the boats afloat.

For a moment they lost control of the boat and it spun crazily, making Slade go dizzy. He felt that at any moment he would be swept into the grey river. The turbulence seemed to last for ever. Then at last it stopped suddenly, and they were in the calm placid river again. The oarsmen of the boats were gasping and coughing as they felt that the danger had passed.

'Did it,' Ray yelled over to Slade's boat.

A second later a bullet sent up a shower of splinters.

'You spoke too soon,' Slade shouted back reaching for his .45.

'They're over there behind them rocks,' Ray shouted, struggling to draw his gun and at the same time control the boat, which was being pulled around by the current into the range of the rifles on the bank.

Slade could see what was happening.

'We ain't in range of them rifles. Keep pulling so we stay out of range,' Slade called over to him. He grasped an oar, and threw his weight against it. Slowly, the boat started to gather speed.

'We're soon gonna be out of range at this rate,' Ray called over the roar of the river.

'Wouldn't count on it,' Slade yelled in surprise.

Following his pointing arm, Ray watched as three men galloped down the river bank, rifles across their saddles, a fourth holding on to the pommel of his saddle, looking as though he had been shot up.

After a few yards, three of the men dismounted, knelt down and started firing at the oarsmen who were getting a mite dispirited on account of how they couldn't send some lead back.

'At least we'll soon be able to give them some of their own medicine,' Slade said. 'The current's carrying us over to the bank.'

'As long as they don't get any better with their shooting,' Ray called over.

'We might get a couple of them.'

'Sure hope so.' Slade levelled his .45 and fired at the fella holding the horses.

The man clutched at his chest and went down. As he dropped the leathers the horses stampeded away. The other outlaws turned to try and stop them, but Slade brought another of them down. That was enough. Ray's boat crunched up on the shale of the bank. Ray and one of the other men jumped out of the boat and sent a couple of shots into the air just to discourage the rest of the outlaws.

'Just keep them hands where I can see them,' Ray yelled at them as he ran towards them. He pulled their guns out of their holsters and tossed them into the river.

'OK, Sheriff, we've had enough,' one of them yelled, throwing up his hands.

Slade and the other man collected the guns and tied them up with a rope they found in one of the boats.

'We can't take them back up the river,' Ray said.

'We might not have to,' Slade said, pointing to the far bank.

The rest of the posse were cantering out of the stand of trees that lined the bank, and splashing into the water. Ray gave them a wave of triumph and pointed to the prisoners.

'Git them horses over here,' Ray shouted across. 'It's shallow enough a hundred yards further down.'

The posse rode downstream and started to splash their way across.

It did not take them long to get to town.

'Just what's bin goin' on?' Ray demanded of Grace Everard when they got back to his office.

She sat looking forlorn in the hard-backed chair.

'It was all Ken's fault,' she began. 'Damn no good cousin. It was his idea. We weren't doing too well at first. He reckoned with everybody in the saloon listening to me singing, it would be a good time for him and his brothers and the other boys to clean out the banks. It was working pretty well, too, until we used too much dynamite on this one, and Dick, my manager, decided to cut Ken and the boys out of the deal. He nearly got them killed, and Dick was getting scared anyway. You saw what happened.'

'You're staring at some hard time in a tough jail,' Ray said angrily. 'All right, put her back in her cell.'

'You've bin damned handy,' Ray said to Slade when his deputy had taken her down to her cell. 'I got room for a deputy. Seems like you know something of this line of work.'

'I know something about this line of work,' Slade admitted. 'But I ain't interested in taking it up again.'

Ray spent a good half-hour in trying to get Slade to change his mind, but in the end he gave it up.

Slade rode out still with no idea where he was going, but he found himself heading south to the border country. He had a spell as a bounty hunter, and payroll guard.

Then one day he knew he had to go back to Blake's Creek.

SIX

The place hadn't changed much, he thought, as he dismounted and tied his horse to the hitch rail outside the saloon. He looked up at the sign. Masters' Palace. It used to be the Last Drop, as he remembered. Brad Masters had come a ways, he thought, going up the steps of the veranda. He eased his hat back and rubbed his face. He put his hand to the batwing doors and was about to push his way in when he heard a muffled drum on the street.

He turned sharply and saw a flat-bed wagon bearing a coffin being hauled down the street by a couple of black horses wearing black plumes that swayed in the light breeze. Behind the wagon several people walked slowly in its wake. One of them was a man who must have been in his early sixties, the other was a girl in her early twenties with a head of bright red hair. Slade wondered if she had a temper to match. Whether she had or not, she was downright pretty. The girl glanced in the direction of the saloon as they passed. A look of hate crossed her face. Slade shrugged it off and pushed into the saloon.

As he did so, the conversation died away, and everybody turned to look at him. One or two scowled in his direction, then went back to their drinking, and ignored Slade.

Slade pushed on to the bar, and signalled the barkeep.

'Beer,' he ordered.

'Beer it is,' the barkeep said and went to one of the pumps.

As he came back with the beer, Slade heard the batwing doors open like somebody was real thirsty. As when he himself had come in, the conversation suddenly died. Slade put down his beer and turned to see who it was. The girl who had been walking behind the wagon with the coffin on it was standing inside the saloon. Her face wore an expression of fury and a whip in her raised hand looked ready to lash out.

'Hold it, Clara,' the barkeep shouted across to her. 'Masters ain't in here.'

'Then where is that murdering snake?' Clara yelled back, threatening those around her with the whip.

'I don't rightly know, Clara, but he ain't in here,' the barkeep assured her.

'Put that whip down Clara, and get out of here,' a tall man at the end of the bar said.

'I'm going nowhere. Not 'til you or somebody tells me where Masters is, you got me, Bentine?'

'You sure take some tellin',' Bentine went on.

'Maybe we should take that whip off her an' give her a taste of it,' a man behind Bentine said.

'Maybe we should,' a fresh voice put in. 'We've got some sympathy for you Clara, but yer old man asked fer it.'

There was a murmur of agreement round the bar. Slade felt something for the girl, maybe he had heard it all before.

Bentine made a lunge for the whip, but Slade dropped his glass and drew. The sound of the shot made everybody look round.

'That's enough,' Slade said.

'The hell with you, mister, whoever you are,' Bentine snarled at him.

'Thanks,' Clara said, having got her temper back and regretting what had happened.

'That's all right,' Slade told her. 'Now why don't you just leave that here, and get back to your ol' man's funeral.'

Clara opened her mouth to speak, but thought better of it. Instead she dropped the whip and quickly went outside.

Slade kept an eye on the rest of the gents, then holstered his gun and followed her out. By the time he got out on to the boardwalk, she was running to where the wagon had stopped and the others were waiting for her.

Slade watched her as she said something to

them. Then they carried on up to Boot Hill. Slade grabbed the arm of a man who was passing.

'See them folks up there,' he said to the surprised individual.

'Yeah, I see them,' came the answer as the man rubbed his arm.

'Who are they?' Slade asked him.

'The young girl, that's Clara Lezard, the old fella, he's Charlie Jennings. The fella in the box, he's William Lezard. Clara's pa. He was the owner of the *Bugle* 'til somebody put a bullet in his back.'

'And just what did this Lezard fella do?'

'He got on the wrong side of Brad Masters, that's what he did. You got any more questions? Because if you haven't I've got somewhere to go.'

'No, I ain't got no more questions,' Slade told him.

The man started to walk away, then turned back.

'Say, don't I know you from somewhere?' he asked.

Slade shook his head. 'Not that I can think of,' he said.

Shaking his head in a puzzled way, the man walked off. Slade grinned to himself.

Some people don't change. Charlie Ford was still the same tubby, helpful fella he had always been.

Once again Slade looked towards the cemetery. They were lowering the coffin into the grave. Clara was leaning on Jennings's shoulder and looked as though she was sobbing. The minister took a step forward and read from his Bible. Slade couldn't hear what he was saying but he had heard the familiar words over the graves of other men.

As the minister was finishing, Slade saw someone else coming into the cemetery and walking towards the grave. The minister stopped what he was saying and turned to face the newcomer.

From what Slade could see another argument was going on over William Lezard's grave. Suddenly, Jennings stepped forward, but the newcomer put his hand on his chest and pushed him away. Jennings staggered back and only the minister's quick reactions stopped him from toppling into the grave.

Clara Lezard stepped forward to do something, but the minister came between her and the newcomer. She simmered down and shook her fists angrily. The man shrugged and laughed as he walked away.

With the coffin in the grave two men stepped forward to fill in the hole, while Clara and Jennings walked back to the cemetery gates.

Slade ground out the stogie and walked towards them. Clara had pulled herself together, Jennings looked white-faced and angry.

'I saw what was going on up there,' Slade told Clara, taking off his hat.

'This is the fella I was telling you about,' she said, nodding at Slade.

'Thanks,' Jennings said. 'I don't know who you are, but if ever the *Bugle* can do anything for you, don't forget to look us up.'

'It seems like the *Bugle* has its own troubles,' Slade said with a wry grin.

'You can say that again,' Jennings said, looking down at Clara.

'We're having a lot of trouble with Brad Masters.'

'The fella that came to the grave,' Slade said.

Clara gave him a puzzled look. 'How come you know Brad Masters?'

'It's a long story. Maybe I'll tell you sometime.'

She stopped for minute. 'I think it was him who shot my father or paid somebody to shoot him.'

'Why?' Slade asked her.

'Masters is involved in every shady deal in this town, that's why, and William Lezard was the kind of newspaperman who would make sure everybody in town knew about it. That's why he got shot.'

'So what about the law? Aren't they going to do something about it?' Slade asked him.

'Not when they're Masters' brother-in-law, they won't,' Clara said angrily.

'I guess I can see your difficulties,' Slade said as he put his hat on again.

'Harry Duncan and his brother-in-law are real close,' Jennings said.

'Maybe I could give you a hand there,' Slade told them.

'You?' Jennings asked in surprise.

'Yeah, me,' Slade said with a serious look on his face.

Clara and Jennings exchanged glances.

'But why should you?' Clara asked him. 'It isn't your fight. You haven't been in town more than half an hour. I saw you riding in just when we started out.'

Slade shrugged. 'I don't like the way things are in this town, and I don't like crooked lawmen.'

'Those sound like a couple of good reasons to me,' Jennings said.

'And me,' Clara added.

'Why don't you walk along with us, and I'll show you where the offices are,' Clara said to him.

'That sounds fine,' Slade replied.

They walked down the street until they came to the general store, then down an alley that led off the street.

'Funny place for a newspaper office,' Slade said when they got to the end of the alley and came to an old house, which looked ready to be pulled down.

'Our office got burned down one night,' Jennings said, seeing Slade looking round.

'Me and Al were working late getting the newspaper together. We were damn lucky to get out,' Clara said when they were inside.

'And the law didn't do anything about it, as you might expect they wouldn't,' Jennings said, reaching for the coffee-pot. 'I'm going to go and fix some coffee.'

Slade went to the door and looked down the alley. It was empty and quiet, but he had seen empty and quiet places before, they didn't always stay that way. Al came back and fixed them all some coffee.

'If yer aimin' to stick around,' he said when they had finished their coffee, 'you might as well do some work.'

'What sort of work have you got in mind?' Slade asked.

'Nothing too demanding,' Clara said to him with a smile.

It was the first time that he had seen her smile, and it made her look even prettier.

'What are you gawping at?' she said colouring up a mite.

Slade laughed. 'Nothing.'

'We ain't got all night,' Al said quickly. 'We've got some newspapers to get out.'

Slade looked at him.

'Tomorrow's edition,' Clara told him. 'It's all printed up and just needs getting out to the customers.'

'Yeah, it's in the cellar,' Al said. 'We'll go down

and get them in a few minutes.'

Slade poured himself another mug of coffee. The night had started to come on, and he walked to the front door. A big yellow moon hung in the sky.

'You'd better come away from that door,' Clara said.

'Why's that?' Slade asked her.

A second later a bullet slammed into the wood over his head. The splinters flew outwards, narrowly missing his face.

Slade dodged back into the house, slamming the door shut as he did so. Another couple of bullets splintered the woodwork.

'They're startin' early,' Al shouted out as a spatter of bullets hit the woodwork.

'You mean you get this all the time?' Slade asked. He drew his gun and smashed the glass in the window.

'Not all the time, just most of it,' Clara shouted across to him from the cover of a set of chairs.

'Can't anybody round here do anything about it?' Slade asked, tossing a shot into the darkness.

'Nobody around here to do anything about it,' Al shouted as a flurry of shots hit the woodwork again.

'The sheriff and Masters are related, like I told you earlier,' Clara said.

Slade took a chance and looked out through

the window into the alley, but could see nothing in the dark.

'They must have been hoping to get lucky,' he told the others.

'Damn near made it a couple of times,' Al called out to him.

'Are you hurt?' Clara asked in a concerned tone.

'No, but if they keep this up they're gonna get lucky sometime,' Al replied.

'Maybe,' Slade said as he checked the loads in his gun.

'You sound real helpful,' Al said.

'Which is the back way out of here?' Slade asked, crawling away from the window.

'Come on, I'll show you,' Clara said.

Slade was surprised to see that she had got a gun from somewhere. He followed her into the kitchen.

'What's out there?' he asked her.

'A back yard, the fence into the alley. Then you just go round the front on to the street. There's another alley just across the road. We figured they're shooting from there.'

'OK, I'll get out there and stop them.' Slade checked the loads in his gun.

Suddenly the girl caught his arm.

'Be careful. They're dangerous,' she said quietly.

'So am I,' he said.

Slade reached up and unlocked the door. He

pulled it open without getting to his feet. The moon shone down into the yard. The yard seemed to be almost empty. A few yards away he could see the fence. It was about waist-high. Reckoning there wasn't anybody watching the rear of the house, Slade got to his feet, and crouching low, ran for the fence. When he got there, he put his free hand on the top of the fence and vaulted into the alley.

The lamps in the neighbouring houses were out. He cat-footed to the end of the alley and looked into the street. From what he could see it was empty. The shooting had made everybody keep his or her head down. Cautiously, he moved down the alley and looked into the street. It was as Clara had told him. Across from the alley where the house was there was another alley. He looked across the street, but could see nothing.

Maybe they weren't in the alley, but in one of the shops next to it. Then he saw slight movement in the shadows. They were there all right. Slade grinned wolfishly. Cat-footing back down the alley, he moved along to the next opening and went to the top. As he did so and looked out, he saw flashes of gunfire, and heard bullets slap into the wood.

Figuring that the men in the alley were concentrating on the house and not on anything else, he sprinted across the street, and got into the alley without being seen. He moved quickly down the alley and round the back of the houses. Slade stopped suddenly when he heard voices speaking quietly in the dark.

'I tell you I saw somebody comin' across the street,' somebody hissed.

'Hank, you didn't see anybody. All you saw was them beer taps. Now, get back to what we're paid to be doin'. We can go down to Masters' place when we've stirred them up a bit more, and git us some more drinks.'

'I'm gonna take a look,' Hank told his partner.

'Stay where you are. We ain't paid to go runnin' round in the dark. It's probably just some stray dog.'

'I'm just gonna make sure,' Hank said finally.

Slade moved against the wall of a house and waited, listening for Hank's footsteps in the dark. He strained to see the outline of Hank's body as it came round the corner. When he was sure he moved quickly and silently, bringing the butt of his pistol down on Hank's head. Hank grunted and buckled at the knees. Slade caught him as he fell. Lowering him to the ground he kicked Hank's gun away, into the dark.

Again, he listened as another shot rang out in the night. Quietly, Slade moved down the alley. He crouched down on one knee and took a look round the corner. Straightaway, he saw Hank's *amigo* leaning against a barrel, levering another round into the breech.

'You find that lost dog?' he was asked as he

crept up behind the man.

'No,' he said quietly. 'But I found you.'

As the man turned in surprise, Slade hit him with the barrel of his gun. Hank's pal went down without a sound.

Slade dragged him to where he had left Hank, then tied them both up with their bandannas. Clara opened the door for him when he got across to the house.

'Are you all right?' she asked him in a whisper.

'I am,' he said, 'but they aren't,' he pointed to the alley.

Al came up behind her.

'You'd best get them down to the sheriff. It won't do any good though. He'll just let them go.'

'I'll go down there anyway, and see what he comes up with. You go and stand over them, and see they don't disappear.'

'OK,' Clara told him.

SEVEN

Slade walked to the end of the alley, and had a look down the street. It was still empty and quiet now. He could remember where the sheriff's office was, and didn't think they would have moved it since.

The light was burning in the office when he got down there. Slade braced himself and went in. At first he thought the place was empty, then he heard a noise from the back somewhere. The door leading to the cells was slightly ajar. Loosening the thong over his gun, he pushed the door open, and looked in. At first he could see nothing, then the shape on the bunk in the nearest cell started to move violently. When he realized what it was, he stepped back into the office and rapped hard on the table.

'You in there anywhere, sheriff?' he shouted out.

There was no answer. Slade was about to call

out again, when he heard some movement in the cell area.

'I'm just coming,' the sheriff called out.

A minute later he appeared in the doorway, fastening the belt round his trousers; his hair was tousled, and he looked as though he had been in a fight. He was a middle-sized man with a weak face. Slade recognized him, but it had been a long time, and he couldn't remember his name.

'I'm Jack Slade,' he began. 'Clara Lezard didn't toss me your name.'

'I'm Jim Duncan,' the sheriff began by saying, then he realized what Slade had said.

'Clara Lezard?' he echoed stupidly.

'Yeah, they buried her old man today. You might have heard about it.'

For a moment Duncan had a stunned expression on his face.

'Yeah, I heard something about it. So what can I do for you?'

'I've got a couple of fellas hogtied down at the old house Clara's using for an office. They were using the office for some target practice,' Slade told him, sitting himself on the edge of the desk.

'I didn't hear no shootin',' Duncan said angrily, flattening his hair with his hand.

'Maybe it was because your mind was elsewhere.' Slade tossed a look at the half-open door.

He had seen a woman pulling on her clothes.

Duncan gave him a hard look, then turned

and pushed the door closed.

'What are you going to do about it?' Slade demanded.

'I guess I'd better get down there,' Duncan said, glancing back at the door he had closed.

'I'll see you down there then. I'll give you five minutes to get down there. If I have to I'll come back for you,' Slade warned him.

Duncan ground his teeth. Slade left him, and wondered who the girl was.

As he walked down the darkened street, he felt the hairs on the back of his neck rising. When he came level with an alley, he sensed the danger. Slade took a dive into the darkened entrance and drew his gun as he went down. A shot followed him into the dark. From the alley across the street, he saw the flash from the gun. Slade rolled on to his belly and tossed a shot back. Another shot followed the first from the dark. Again Slade returned the shot, and waited, but whoever was doing the shooting had had enough. Slade heard the sound of running as he got to his feet.

They were still waiting for him when he got back to the house. Clara hurried to him when she saw him coming.

'We heard more shooting. What happened?'

'Somebody tried to save the sheriff a walk down here,' he said.

The girl gave him a quizzical look. He told her about the shooting.

'Who do you reckon it was?' she asked him.

'They didn't stop to introduce themselves,' he said.

'Are you all right?' she asked him.

Slade nodded. It was a strange feeling to have somebody caring about what happened to him. Not since he was last in this town, and he had been very young then. Or maybe just Jethro and his wife.

As he was thinking Duncan clumped into the alley.

'Where are they?' he demanded.

Al came out of the house.

'I've got them in here, Sheriff,' he said, pointing over his shoulder.

They led Duncan into the house. Hank and his pal were sitting on the floor in the hall looking pretty damned miserable.

'You know these two gents?' Slade asked him.

Duncan said nothing for a moment, then shook his head.

'No, I ain't seen them round town,' he said.

Watching his face, Slade knew that he was lying.

'What are you goin' to do with them?' he asked the sheriff.

'You got any witnesses?' Duncan demanded.

'Only me,' Slade answered.

'That ain't good enough,' Duncan told him. 'I need an independent witness.'

Slade and the others were getting angry.

'The least you can do is lock them up. Then, in the morning, we'll see,' Al put in.

Duncan glared at him, his weak bottom lip quivering as he did so. Saliva ran down to his chin.

'Are you going to do your job?' Clara snapped at him. 'Or do I run an extra edition saying that you let these two fellas go?'

Duncan looked at her as though he wanted to slap her.

'All right,' he said reluctantly. 'I'll take them in, but you've got to get me some hard evidence by morning.'

'OK, you two get on your feet,' Slade told them.

Before they could move he grabbed them by the scruffs of their necks and pulled them to their feet.

'Go easy,' Hank yelled at him.

'Keep it quiet,' Al Jennings said. 'You're gonna have the whole town awake.'

'I'll just walk down to the jail with you to make sure you get there in one piece,' Slade said to Duncan.

Sheriff Duncan looked as though he didn't like the sound of this, but he had no choice.

Slade pushed them towards the door. They walked up the alley in silence and along to the jail. Duncan let them in.

'I'll go and lock them up,' he said to Slade.

Slade sat in the chair in front of Duncan's

desk. He waited while the sheriff locked up the two men.

'What's your play in all this?' Duncan asked him when he came back.

'I ain't rightly sure,' Slade told him. Maybe it was time to lay his cards on the table.

'What do you mean, you ain't rightly sure?' Duncan took a bottle of whiskey out of the desk drawer and pulled the cork.

'I was passing by, and I wondered if things had changed since I was last here,' Slade said as the sheriff poured himself some of the whiskey into a mug. He didn't offer Slade any.

'You've been in town before?' Duncan said, putting the mug to his mouth.

'Sort of. I used to live here. Me and my family.'

Duncan stopped drinking and looked hard at him.

'I've changed a lot,' Slade told him.

The sheriff's eyes narrowed as he tried to place Slade. Then the recognition came into them.

'You're young Jack Slade, ain't you,' he said, his face changing colour.

'Yeah, that's me,' Slade said.

Duncan put the mug down with a thump. His face had gone ashen. The hand that had held the mug was shaking.

'Look, Jack. I wasn't the sheriff then,' he said shakily. 'The old man who was sheriff, he's dead now. Killed chasing some bank-robbers out near Black Wells.'

'I figured he might be,' Slade said, reaching over and taking the bottle from Duncan. 'I never figured he'd be any good after he let the lynch-mob kill my pa, and he let them come after me.'

Duncan licked his lips. The sweat broke out on his face.

'Jack, like I said, I never had anything to do with that.' By now, he was almost gabbling.

'Hell, you weren't much older than me, and I was only a kid,' Slade told him taking a drink from the mug.

'Then why did you come back? There ain't any good memories here for you.' Duncan poured more whiskey into the mug and swallowed it down.

'I came back to see your sister, Jacqueline. We used to be close. Remember?'

Again, Duncan's face became white. The whiskey he had drunk had put some of the colour back into it.

'What happened to her?'

Duncan swallowed. 'She married Brad Masters,' he said slowly.

Slade sat up straight in the chair. That had really shaken him.

'Masters? She married Masters?'

'Yeah, a couple of years after you left,' Duncan was having difficulty with his words.

'How is she?' Slade asked him.

'She's fine. They live out at . . .' again he stopped, having trouble with his words. 'They built a place near your old man's.'

'Pa's old place?' Slade echoed the words.

'Yeah, a couple of miles away from the original place near the river. I think maybe Masters did it to get even with your pa, for not selling it to him when he wanted to buy it.'

It was Slade's turn to go white. Masters had always wanted his pa's place, and his pa hadn't wanted to sell it, but Masters had got hold of it anyway.

'What are you going to do, Jack?' he heard Duncan ask him.

Slade didn't answer for a spell.

'I'll think on it,' he said finally as he got up.

'If you decide to go after Masters give me plenty of time to get out of town,' Duncan said.

'I sure as hell will,' Slade told him, watching him drain his whiskey. He got up to go.

'Are you all right?' Clara asked him when he got back to the office. 'You've been gone the hell of a while.'

'Yeah, I'm fine,' Slade lied.

Slade told them what had passed between him and Duncan.

Clara and Al looked at each other. They shook their heads as they went into the house.

Slade watched them go. He stood watching the stars for a few minutes, and thinking of the past. Maybe that was why he had come back after all this time. Square things with Masters, and get it out of his system for ever. Or maybe he didn't know, and never would.

Back in the office Duncan went down to see Hank and his *amigo*.

'Don't know why yer wastin' everybody's time,' Hank said flopping down on the warm bunk. 'Yer just gonna have to let us out of here when Masters gets to find out about it.'

'Yeah I know,' Duncan replied, putting the keys to the cell on his belt. 'But stay put until he does that.'

Brad Masters was in the back room of Masters' Palace, counting the night's takings. He looked up sharply as the door flew open. Mike Lester came in.

'Them boys shoot the place up?' Masters asked him.

Lester sat down opposite his boss.

'Yeah, they shot it up,' he replied, eyeing the whiskey bottle at Masters' elbow.

'Then why are you looking so hot and bothered?' Masters reached for the whiskey bottle and a glass.

'Some fella got the drop on them and got the sheriff to take them down to the jail.'

Masters threw him an angry look, then pushed the glass across to him.

'I'll go down and get them out of there.'

Lester picked up the glass and put the whiskey down in one.

'Say you got any idea who this fella was?' Masters asked him.

'No,' Lester said. 'Maybe Duncan can tell you. Him and this fella had a long talk while the fella was in there. I took a shot at him on the way back but missed him.'

'OK, leave Duncan to me,' Masters said.

'OK, boss,' Lester got to his feet.

Masters watched him go then raked the uncounted money into a drawer. When he had finished he stood up, put on his hat and went through the saloon to the street.

'Where've you been?' he asked Amy when he saw her heading for the saloon. 'You should be in there working.'

'I've bin working for you with that no good *amigo*,' she snarled at him.

Masters laughed. 'Sure likes his free time with you, doesn't he?'

Amy scowled and hurried into the saloon.

'Heard you've arrested a couple of the boys,' Masters said when he got down to the jail.

'You'd better forget about your boys,' Duncan said, handing him a glass of whiskey.

'Why should I do that?' Masters asked angrily.

'Because you might have real trouble. You know who that fella was that brought them in?'

'No,' Masters said taking a drink of the whiskey, and calming down.

Duncan watched him.

'Remember old man Slade? The fella that you got lynched for something he didn't do?'

Masters felt uneasy. 'What has a dead old man got to do with me?'

'He had a kid, remember? That's the fella that brought your boys in.'

Masters felt his face tighten, and his body go cold. Duncan watched him with a feeling of smug satisfaction.

'I'm going to have to do something about it,' Masters told him.

'Well, make sure I'm out of the way,' Duncan said.

'I'll make sure you're out of the way,' Masters said. 'I'm gonna have to do something about it, though.'

'I know you will, or this fella will do something about it.'

'He'd better be good,' Masters sneered.

Duncan shrugged and poured himself another glass.

Masters drained his, put it down on the sheriff's desk, and went out to get hold of Lester.

EIGHT

Slade and Al had hauled the fresh copies up out of the cellar where Clara had put them for safe-keeping.

'Are you gonna help us get them delivered?' Al asked Slade.

'Sure,' Slade replied, picking up an armful of the newspapers.

Clara came out of the back room, slinging a bag over her shoulder.

'You coming with us?' Slade asked her.

'No, I'm going feeding the ducks,' she said with a sarcastic grin. 'Let's go.'

Slade slung the bag that Al had given him over his shoulder and headed for the door.

Outside there were a few people already on the street.

'Everybody you meet,' Clara said to Slade, 'you give them one of these.'

She thrust one into the hand of the man who ran the general store.

'Thanks,' he said tipping his hat and opening the paper to read the headlines.

'Now all the houses along this street,' Clara said to Slade.

He left her to cross the street. Now they were in the part of town that had been newly built. He went up a path and left one on the veranda.

Masters had arrived back at the saloon. He had got in through the back, it being closed up after the night's business had finished.

'Find Lester and get him over here,' he told one of his barkeeps.

'Right, boss,' the barkeep said and went to find Lester.

He found Lester over at the boarding-house getting ready to have some breakfast before he turned in.

He gave the barkeep a sour look when he told him what he wanted.

'OK,' he said. 'I'll get over there.'

The barkeep went back across the street and told Masters. A few minutes later Lester got there.

'What d'ya want, boss?' he asked.

'I want a little problem solving. The one you should have solved last night.'

'The fella that turned Hank in?' Lester asked.

'Yeah, that fella that turned Hank in,' Masters said, turning over a rasher of bacon on his plate. 'Him and that stupid bitch will be out delivering the next edition of her lying paper. Get her too if you can,' Masters said, cutting up the bacon. 'Wait for them at the house. Don't worry about Duncan. He won't interfere. If he does give him a bullet.'

'OK, boss,' Lester said eagerly. He got up out of the chair.

Outside, it was already getting hot. Lester walked down past the saloon, and crossed the street, hefting the gun on his hip. He felt good, real good about it.

He walked down the alley, picking his spot. The way he figured it, they would come up to the front door and go inside. Just before they got to the house there was an old run-down shed, that nobody used for anything. Walking back, he tried the door. It opened at his second push, and he went inside. The place was dark and smelly.

A dirty window looked out on to the alley. Lester cleaned it off with his sleeve, after which he was able to look out clearly on to the alley. He broke open his .45 and checked the loads. Then he closed it, put it back in the holster and settled himself down to wait.

'Makes things a whole lot easier with an extra pair of hands,' Clara said, when they reached the alley.

Slade felt uneasy.

'You wait here for a spell,' he said looking at the shed.

Clara and Al gave him a questioning look. Slade walked a few yards ahead of them. He saw the window that Lester had cleaned. Slade turned sharply, and ran for the door of the shed, his gun in his hand.

He kicked the door open, then hit the floor. Lester's shot winged over his head. Slade fired at the gun-flash. The bullet smashed into the wall of the shed.

Clara and Al ran back into the street.

Slade ran among the stuff in the shed as another shot whined out into the alley.

Lester was pressed back against the wall. Suddenly waiting in the shed wasn't such a good idea. He hadn't left himself a way out, and Slade was faster than he had reckoned him to be. The place was full of old chairs and tables. As silently as he could, he moved round them.

'OK,' Slade yelled. 'Toss the gun away, and go out into the light where I can see you.'

Lester ignored him and threw a shot his way. It went wide.

Again Slade saw the flash and threw a shot back at it. It splintered the wood of one of the tables and tore a chunk out of Lester's arm. He felt the warm blood running down to his hands, making his gun slippery in his fingers.

'I know I got you, so be sensible and come on out,' Slade yelled to him.

'Come and get me,' Lester shouted back, trying to stop the blood with his bandanna.

'Have it your way, fella,' Slade called over to him. 'I don't know who you are but I don't figure I've got a quarrel with you. Just come on out.'

'You go to hell, Slade,' Lester called out.

Slade knew that the man was never going to come out. He started forwards, thumbing back the hammer of his .45. The motes of dust were rising into the light that came in from the window.

Lester moved round a stack of tables, trying to keep from being silhouetted against the window. He knocked against a table and cursed under his breath. Slade turned sharply to his left, ready for his opponent to fire or make a break for it. Nothing happened. He moved in the direction of the sound. A chair and table hit the floor with a crash. Lester stood up to fire. Slade saw him for a second and fired first. The bullet slammed into Lester's heart, flinging him against the wall. His body slid down to the floor leaving a line of blood against the wall as he went down.

Slade put the gun back into the holster and went outside. Clara and Al were coming back into the alley.

'We heard that last shot,' Al said. 'We figured that was it.'

'Yeah, that was it,' Slade said.

'I guess somebody had better go an' get Duncan,' Al said, wiping the sweat off his face.

He turned and headed for the sheriff's office.

Slade and Clara watched him go until he disappeared round the corner.

'I'll go in and make a pot of coffee while we wait for Duncan to get here,' Clara said anxiously.

'You don't sound any too happy,' Slade said to her as they went to the house.

'Sometimes I ask myself, is it all worth it,' she answered tiredly.

'I thought you newspaper people were meant to be dedicated.' Slade held the door open for her.

'We are,' she said snappishly, which Slade put down to the strain of what had happened.

'I'm sorry,' he said.

'It doesn't matter,' she replied, yawning, and headed for the kitchen.

She went to make the coffee and it wasn't long before Duncan arrived, wearing an angry expression.

'What the hell's been going on?' he demanded of Slade.

'Somebody's been using us for target practice,' Slade said to him, watching the lawman's face.

'Did you get a look at him?' Duncan asked.

'No, but you can,' Slade rasped at him.

Duncan gave him a questioning look.

'He's down there with a bullet in him.' Slade pointed at the old shed.

Duncan turned and walked out of the house.

Slade gave him a couple of seconds, then followed him.

'Know him?' he asked when they both got there.

At first Duncan said nothing.

'I said, do you know him?' repeated Slade.

'He's a fella called Lester,' Duncan said slowly, his mouth dry.

'That doesn't sound as if that's all you know about him.'

'He works for Masters,' Duncan said.

'All right, where do I find Masters? Leave it between him and me. I'll give him a chance to turn himself in, but I don't reckon he will.'

'Fine. Like I said to him, just leave me out of it.'

Looking at the sheriff, Slade saw that he was making an effort to control his fear.

'All right, just tell me where he is, and I'll take my quarrel out of here.'

'He's probably back at his ranch by now. You'll most likely find him there,' Duncan said looking mighty relieved.

'Thanks, Sheriff. If this pans out, you won't be seeing me again,' Slade said quietly.

'I hope not,' Duncan said, sounding relieved.

Out in the alley, Slade took a good deep lung-ful of fresh air to get the smell of death out of his lungs. At the far end of the alley, Clara was standing in the doorway of the house watching him.

'That coffee's brewed,' she said.

'I guess I'll have time for a mug before I go looking for Masters,' he told her, noting the disappointed look in her face.

'Are you likely to be back this way?' she asked him.

'I don't know,' he told her honestly. 'It depends on how it goes with Masters. I just don't know.'

They went into the house where she fixed up the coffee. Al had gone off somewhere, and Clara didn't seem to have too much to say.

When he had finished his coffee, Slade went outside to saddle up his horse which he had brought up from the livery stable the night before. Clara watched him mount up and ride out without a word.

Slade headed out towards his old home, and swung off to the left where the trail met the river. From a low rise in the ground he surveyed the house that Masters had built. Masters had done well enough for himself, he thought. Newly built house, some good land and his girl.

Slade spurred the horse down the trail, until he came to the gate. He dismounted, pushed it open and let the horse walk the rest of the way. He hitched it at the post outside the house and walked up to the door.

After he had knocked, he waited until he heard footsteps in the hall. He put his hand on his gun, and waited for the door to open.

'Yes?' she asked not recognizing him. 'Who

are you and what do you want?'

'Don't you remember me?' he asked her, taking his hand from his gun.

She looked at him, and screwed up her eyes, as if she was making an effort to remember him. It took a while for it to sink in.

'Jack,' she said slowly as the colour drained from her face.

He moved forward quickly to catch her as she fell. Slade carried her into the parlour and laid her on the sofa.

He went to the kitchen door and looked inside. It was empty.

'Anybody home?' he called from the foot of the stairs. Again there was no answer. Back in the parlour, Jacqueline was just starting to come round.

Slade went over to her and helped her sit up. The colour was slowly returning to her cheeks.

'Where is he?' he asked her.

'Brad?' she asked him. 'He went back to town.'

'You know what he's been doing? He's had William Lezard killed. He's sent one of his hired guns to kill me,' he told her roughly.

'I know what he is, but I didn't believe he's had Clara's father killed,' she gasped.

'Somebody tried to kill me earlier on. A fella called Lester. Maybe it was him.'

'Maybe, I don't know. My husband is in a lot of dirty deals. If he did do that, he'd use Lester.'

'And I've a good idea that he set my pa up for that lynching.' Slade was suddenly running out of patience. He took her roughly by the shoulders and shook her.

When she started to sob, he stopped, angry and ashamed of himself. Hell, it wasn't her fault.

'Help me stand up,' she said to him.

Slade put his arms under her, and helped her get to her feet.

'I'm sorry,' she gasped as soon as she felt better. 'I didn't know that he had set your father up for that lynching.'

'He wanted Pa's land. All right, where is he?' Slade asked her, his voice rising with his anger.

'He's gone back to town,' she said huskily.

'I'm going back, and I'm going to kill him if he doesn't turn himself in.' Slade told her roughly.

'We thought you were dead. The last we heard you were scouting for Custer on the Platte, and when word came through about him getting killed . . .' she broke off with a shrug.

'I know, you figured I was with him,' he said, feeling a little pity for her.

Jacqueline did not answer. Figuring that there was nothing else to be said, Slade went to his horse and rode back to town.

He found Clara and Al at the house getting the paper ready for putting out on the streets later that week. Clara looked up at him in surprise when he walked in.

'We didn't expect to see you again,' she said.

'Masters came back to town, just as I got to the ranch,' he said quickly.

'Well, you might not get him,' Al said, checking a sheet of paper.

'How's that?' Slade asked him.

'I was down at the sheriff's office. They've sent a federal marshal into town. Place is getting a bad name. I don't think he'd stand for another killing no matter how well intentioned.'

'Damn it,' exploded Slade.

'If you want Masters for your pa's lynching and the robbery on the stage,' Clara put in helpfully, 'there used to be a man called Jimmy Cabot. Him and Masters were always pretty thick. Cabot left town not too long back. Maybe he knows something,' Clara said.

'Maybe,' Slade said. 'You don't happen to know where he went?'

Clara thought for a moment. 'As I recall, he had a place near Twin Bends. Cabot liked his privacy and it's pretty private around there.'

'Twin Bends. I know the place. I used to do some fishing up there when I was a kid. I'll be heading up that way, especially if he can clear my pa, and put Masters behind bars.'

'You're going up there after him, to see if he'll testify against Masters?' Clara asked.

'Yeah. I can't see Masters coming back here,' Slade told her.

'No, I suppose not,' she agreed. 'Just be careful.'

'I will,' he told her as he walked out.

It was about mid-morning when Slade rode out and headed up to Twin Bends. He remembered the place well. As he had told Clara, he used to go up there with his pals to fish and swim in the easy-flowing river. They used to spend the weekends up there among the tall pine trees. They would go down to the edge of the river for a spell and watch the fish, then toss in their lines and catch a few for supper.

The arrival of the marshal had taken Masters by surprise, although he realized that it shouldn't have done. First he'd had to get Lester to kill that old fool Lezard, then his daughter had taken over the running of the newspaper, then Jack Slade had come back to town. He had the feeling that things were closing in on him.

Having left Duncan in his office, he walked down to his saloon, and took the bottle of whiskey from the desk drawer and had a couple of stiff drinks to help him along.

'How are things out there, Jimmy?' he asked his head barkeep.

'It was a bit slow last night, on account of the shooting,' Jimmy told him.

'If anybody wants me I've gone back to the ranch. I might be leaving the territory for a while. If I do, keep an eye on things. I'll be coming back in the near future.'

'OK, boss,' Jimmy called to him and watched

him go out to his office.

In his office Masters opened the safe and ran his eyes over the contents: $10,000. Wedge by wedge he pulled the money out and stuffed it into a saddle-bag he kept permanently in his office. This done, he fastened up the saddle-bag and tossed it over his shoulder. Whistling, he went out to the back alley where he had left his horse.

Once in the saddle he rode out of town and up towards his ranch. Most of the hands were out clearing up the damage and rounding up the cattle that had strayed through the broken fences during a freak storm that had lashed the range. He dismounted and tethered his horse to the hitch rail, then walked up to the front door. The minute he opened it he knew that something was wrong.

'Jacqueline,' he called out. 'Jacqueline.'

He walked through to the parlour. There was nobody there. Masters went upstairs to the bedroom. Cautiously, he opened the door. Jacqueline was sitting at her dressing-table.

'Didn't you hear me call out?' he asked roughly, pulling her round by her shoulders.

'Yes,' she said dully. 'I heard you.'

'Then why didn't you answer me?' he demanded.

She just looked at him. Masters shook her.

'He's been here looking for you,' she said.

'Who's been here?' he demanded, shaking her again.

'Jack Slade. I think he's going to kill you,' she said, moving away from him as he let her go.

'What have you told him?' Masters asked, following her to the window.

'I didn't tell him anything. He just wanted to know where you were so he could kill you . . .' Her voice trailed away as she saw the look in his eyes.

'You stupid bitch,' he yelled at her.

Masters brought back his hand to slap her. She twisted out of his grip, but sprawled on the floor. He caught her by her long blonde hair. He slapped her again and again until she stopped moving. He stood over her body breathing heavily.

Masters bent over his wife. She had stopped breathing. The rage took him again. He shook her again and again.

'Wake up, you stupid bitch,' he yelled.

He let go of her. She flopped back on to the floor. Masters cursed her and his temper.

What the hell had she told Slade, he asked himself? Had she told him about Cabot and his part in the framing of his father. Cabot, he hadn't seen him round town for a spell. Maybe he was up in his cabin. He liked getting away from things for while.

There was only Cabot who could pin anything on him.

Cabot would have to follow her, he decided. Masters ran from the house. He climbed into the

114

saddle and headed his horse out of the yard. One of his men who had come back for some grub from the cookhouse watched him heading out towards Twin Bends. He grabbed some food from the table, pushed it into his saddle-bags and went back to work.

NINE

Jack Slade was headed up that way. His hopes were high for getting Cabot to testify against Masters. He pushed on through the heat of the day, the ground slowly rising as he rode. It had been a long time since he had been up to Twin Bends. Not since the day when his pa had been framed by Masters. He rode on, his anger rising.

Jimmy Cabot was lying half-awake, half-drunk on the bunk in his cabin. His mouth was dry and hot, his head felt as though somebody had been using it to stomp on. He couldn't remember an awful lot of what had happened the night before when he and the boys had tied one on. Slick Dillon was a mean son-of-a-bitch. and a bank-robber and a killer, but he could sure organize a party, he grinned to himself. All they'd been short of was a couple of dancing girls.

Yesterday, they had hit the bank in Black Falls, and Dillon had started shooting when they came out of the bank. There hadn't been any need for it. They were getting away all nice and friendly-like, then Dillon just started throwing lead at a couple of passers-by who didn't know that a robbery was going on. A kid went down holding his belly; a woman took one in the head. By that time, the sheriff and a couple of deputies were on the street, trying to bring them down. Instead they had been brought down, along with a couple more townsfolk.

The gang had hightailed it out of town, and up into the hills to their hideout. That night, they had split the loot, and finished off a few bottles of red-eye. Part-way through the night Cabot knew that he had had enough of the life of an outlaw and a killer, and he was getting out. Quietly, he saddled up his horse and rode out before any of them knew what had happened.

At his cabin, he went inside and kicked the door closed behind him. Two more bottles of red-eye were stashed away somewhere. Half-drunk, he rooted them out, and sat staring at the wall, steadily drinking them until he passed out.

This morning he felt no differently about things. He wasn't going to turn himself in. He was just going to move on and try to forget it all.

When he got up off the floor everything spun, and he had to catch hold of the edge of the old table to stop himself going over again, Cabot shook his head like a big shaggy bear, but that didn't make him feel any better.

When he got outside, he dunked his head in the barrel of icy mountain water. He held himself down, then came up like a whale, coughing and gasping for air. That made him feel better. His head felt clearer.

His brown bay chomped at the grass, sniffed the air, and then looked at Cabot. Cabot hitched his pants up round his belly, and went over to the horse. He patted it gently of the side of the neck, unhitched it, and got into the saddle. Cabot headed along the trail, taking care to avoid Dillon's hideout. The boys would still be asleep, snoring off their fat heads.

Masters, now that his temper had cooled a mite, was making good time up country. At the top of a rise he hauled on the leathers and looked down. Like Slade, he found the place quiet and empty. He was only a couple of miles from Cabot's place. With any luck, he'd be there in a couple of hours. He pushed the horse along steadily, until he came to a bend in the trail. Suddenly two masked men came out of the undergrowth, brandishing their .45s at him.

'Hold it there, friend,' one of them said to him.

'What do you want?' Masters asked, keeping his temper in check.

'Not your company,' came back the sharp answer.

'I ain't got a heap in my wallet,' Masters called back, his fingers fidgeting with the fresh air.

'Let's take a look-see,' was the answer. 'Toss it down and take it slow and careful. You won't get another chance.'

Slowly Masters reached into the inside pocket of his coat and took out his wallet, letting it fall to the ground.

Masters watched as the man's companion reached down and picked up the wallet. His fat, stubby fingers flipped it open and lifted out the wad of bills.

'Would you look at that?' the outlaw sang out, waving the greenbacks in the air. 'A right lucky day for us, ain't it fella?' he said to Masters. 'Dillon's gonna feel a heap better when he sees this.'

'Slick Dillon?' Masters asked him quickly.

'Yeah, Slick Dillon. Why, you got something against the boss?' the hardcase with the gun asked threateningly.

Masters laughed.

'I didn't know Slick was back in this part of the country. No, I ain't got anything against old Slick. It would be a real pleasure seeing him again after all this time.'

The man with the gun looked up at Masters.

'You know the boss?' the man asked.

'From way back.' Masters told him with a grin. 'You boys gonna take me to him?'

The men looked at him suspiciously for minute.

'OK,' the one with the gun said. 'But if this is a play for time, we're gonna put a bullet in yer hide. You understand?'

'I understand,' Masters said with a smile.

The man with the gun put it away and walked into the undergrowth again. He came back a minute later leading a couple of horses.

'OK, let's git,' he said, handing the leathers of one of the horses to his *amigo*.

They rode off the trail and started heading downwards. Soon Masters could hear thunder in the distance, and they came to a waterfall.

'We're here. I'll lead your horse,' Masters was told by the outlaw who had relieved him of his wallet.

He handed the leathers over to him, and followed him along the trail. The man suddenly veered off to his left and began to ride his horse along the river. He pressed close to the bank as he led Masters behind the waterfall. The place was dark, with only the roaring of the water to be heard.

'Neat, ain't it?' he said as they went deeper into the underground chamber.

A light suddenly appeared out of the darkness.

'Who's that?' a voice snarled.

'It's us, you dumb-cluck, who did you think it was?'

'I don't know, but me an' the boys are a mite hung over this morning,' the voice, dry with the whiskey, continued.

'You sound as though the robbery didn't go so great,' Masters heard one of the men shout above the roar of the waterfall.

'Slick got trigger-happy, and we did some killin',' was the reply.

'Well, we brought an old acquaintance for him,' he was told.

'Jes' follow me,' came the answer.

Masters saw a cabin in the dark, and followed the men inside.

Slick Dillon stood near the back wall, his face ruddy with the drink. He looked across at Masters, then looked again.

'Brad Masters, by all that's holy,' he bawled, then crossed the room, and clasped Masters round the body in a bear-hug.

'Go easy,' laughed Masters. 'You're behaving like a crazy grizzly bear.'

'It's just so damn good to see you again.' Dillon laughed, reached for a bottle of whiskey and put it to his coarse lips.

When he had finished, he handed it to Masters, who did the same.

'What brings you here?' he asked Masters.

'I'm lookin' fer a fella,' Masters answered him.

'That's funny, we've just lost one. We think he's skipped. We ain't too bothered about that, but he might just bring the law up here,' Dillon said, taking another pull at the bottle. 'Your fella got a name?'

'Yeah, Cabot,' Masters said.

Dillon and a couple of his boys let out a loud guffaw.

'That's the fella we're lookin' for,' he said. 'What's he done to you?'

'He could get me hanged,' Masters said grimly, fingering his neck.

'You don't say.' Dillon laughed. 'You won't find him up here. What's it worth to you if we find him for you?'

Masters thought about it.

'Five thousand dollars is what it's worth,' he said seriously. 'Less what was in my wallet.'

Dillon looked at him, then laughed.

'OK. Mike, what was in that wallet?'

'Two hundred dollars,' Mike said.

'Liar,' Masters said. 'It was three hundred dollars.'

'Yeah, my mistake,' Mike agreed. 'Three hundred dollars.'

'Don't go making any more mistakes like that,' Masters warned him.

'Same old tight-fisted Masters,' Dillon laughed.

'We got a deal?' Masters asked.

'Sure we got a deal. How long will it take you

to get the money up here?' Dillon said, tossing the bottle to Masters.

'Tomorrow. I'm gonna have to rest my horse, and get some rest myself.'

'OK, boys, show Masters where he can get some sleep.'

Cabot had ridden away from his shack, and was heading down country, the river on his left. He was starting to feel bad. It wasn't the whiskey. It was something deeper. Something that had been eating at his craw for a spell. He hadn't done a heap with his life and when they'd hit the bank and he'd got to drinking with the boys, he realized how low he had sunk. He hawked and spat on to the trail.

Maybe the time had come for him to find somewhere to start again. His pa had been a God-fearing man; he'd always told him that God would listen if the repentance was sincere, and Cabot's repentance this morning was sincere. Cabot swayed a little in his saddle as he rode.

Clara Lezard was worrying a mite. She didn't know what she was worrying about, not unless you counted Slade, and he was becoming a big thing in her life, she realized. It wasn't that that was worrying her, it was something, she felt, to do with Masters. She hadn't seen him for a while. She stood at the door of the old house.

'Al,' she shouted, 'I'm going up to Masters' place, something doesn't set right,' she told him.

'Is that wise? Masters is a bad piece of news,' Al said.

'You think I don't know that,' she snapped.

'Yeah, I know you know that,' Al replied.

'I'm sorry, Al, I didn't mean that.'

'I know you didn't,' he said putting his hand on her shoulder.

If he had married and had a girl, he would have wanted her to be like Clara. Full of sass, but still a woman.

Clara walked away from the house and down to the livery stable.

'Got my horse?' she asked old man Parker, the owner of the livery.

'Sure have, Clara,' he said, kicking at the dust. He walked into the stable to saddle the horse and bring it out.

He watched her climb into the saddle and felt the same thing that Al had felt. She rowelled the horse and headed up to Masters' place.

She rode hard up the rocky trail and soon found herself at the gate of the ranch. One of the ranch hands held the leathers of her horse as she got down.

'Is Masters here?' she asked him.

'Dunno, Clara. Me and Jess, we just got back. We were about to go up to the house and see him ourselves.'

Clara felt a rush of anger as she walked towards the house, with the others following her. She rapped loudly on the door and waited. No answer. Impatiently, she rapped again.

'Don't look like he's at home,' Jess said.

'Jacqueline should be,' Clara snapped.

She twisted the knob and pushed the door open.

'Seems somebody's bin having a war.' Jess whistled as he followed her in.

'I'm going to try upstairs,' Clara said to them.

She ran up the stairs and looked in all the rooms, until she found Jacqueline.

'Up here,' she called down from the top step.

The two men ran up the stairs.

'In there,' Clara yelled, pointing them to the bedroom when they got to the top of the stairs.

Jess brushed past her and looked down at Jacqueline.

'She's had the hell of a beating,' he said, as he bent down.

'No need to get a doctor,' Clara said quietly, kneeling beside him. 'She's dead.'

She and Jess got up and covered Jacqueline with a small rug.

'Go into town and get Duncan out here,' she said, opening the door for him.

She watched as he mounted up and galloped out of the yard.

'Anybody any idea where Masters would have gone?' she asked the remaining ranch hand.

'I was in the cookhouse when he got back here. Saw him head out in the direction of Twin Bends.'

'Twin Bends?' Clara echoed.

'Yeah,' he replied.

That was where Slade was headed. Clara looked round to her horse.

'Tell Duncan he's gone up to Twin Bends, and I'm going to follow him,' she said. She climbed into the saddle and rowelled her horse. She pushed the horse hard to get to Twin Bends.

Slade had rested his horse and shot a rabbit for something to eat. He sat picking at the bones, wishing that he had some coffee to help it down. The food made him feel a whole lot better. Getting up, he stretched his body. Cabot's place wasn't too far away as he remembered. He got into the saddle and headed out.

He got to Cabot's cabin a couple of hours later. From the edge of the clearing it didn't look as though there was anybody there. He got out of the saddle and took out his gun, then he cat-footed towards the door, keeping a careful look out for Cabot.

As he got to the door, he could see that it was open. He pushed his way inside and found nothing. He put his gun away and looked round the place. Outside, he examined the ground. There were numerous tracks leading away from the place. He walked his horse down the trail, looking at the tracks. After a while he mounted up, and started out after Cabot.

Cabot hauled on the leathers of his horse and got down. The place had a peaceful air about it. He looked up and down the street. Not too many people about. It might be the place to make another start, but then maybe not. It wasn't too far away from a couple of places that Slick and the boys had been raising hell in. He'd get himself something to eat, then carry on until he was far enough away to settle.

He went into the small eating-place and found a table near the back. The cook came over a few minutes later.

'Want something, bud?' he asked Cabot.

'Just something to eat. Nothing fancy.'

'We don't do anything fancy,' the cook told him, and walked back to the kitchen.

Cabot yawned and leaned back in his chair. It had been a long time since he had eaten, especially something that had been properly cooked and didn't look as though it had crawled in from the street. He yawned again.

'This is the best we do,' the sour-faced cook told him as he put the plate down in front of him.

The food was ham and eggs.

'You want some coffee?' Cabot was asked.

'Yeah,' he said, reaching for his eating-irons.

'Comin' up,' the cook told him.

Cabot laid into the ham and eggs.

'Yeah, he's one of them,' the cook said to his pal when he got back to the kitchen.

'You sure, Bert? The sheriff ain't going to be any too pleased if we try to arrest the wrong fella.'

'Mitch, I was as close as I am to you when they walked into the bank. He had no mask on, no nothing. You see him, a big shaggy bear of a man. Now you go an' get the sheriff, while I keep an eye on him.'

Mitch cast a doubtful look at Cabot then turned and went out. He walked down to the sheriff's office and went in. Frank Harris was trying to swat a fly that was flying round just out of his reach.

'Somethin' the matter, Mitch?' he asked, putting down the piece of wood that he was going for the fly with.

'Yeah, Bert sent me down,' said Mitch.

'One of his customers upped and died on him, have they?' Harris said, swatting at the fly.

'No, he reckons one of his customers was in on that bank job over at Clear Springs last month.'

Harris leaned forward in his desk. 'He sure?' he asked, pushing the fly-swat out of the way.

'Way Mitch puts it, he is. Reckons this fella came in with the rest of them large as life.'

Harris paused to consider this.

'Where's Jacko?' he asked.

'Last time I saw him, he was over at Jim's getting his locks trimmed,' Mitch replied, leaning over the desk.

'You go get him and bring him over here.'

'Sure. You gonna ambush this fella?' Mitch asked with an air of suppressed excitement.

'Hell no, we're just gonna let him eat his fill and ride out,' Harris said in an exasperated way.

'Seems a damned strange way of doing things.' Mitch's voice became puzzled.

'Damn it, get yer sorry ass out of here and get Jacko over. Make sure nobody sees you,' Harris said, reaching into the desk for his spare .45.

Mitch left the office in a hurry.

He ran across the street to where he had last seen Jacko. He opened the door of the barber's. Jacko was sitting in the chair, with a heap of white lather on his bloated face.

'Yeah, what do you want?' he asked, after he had wiped the lather off his face.

'Harris's got some trouble. He wants you over at his office,' Mitch said.

'OK, I'm comin'.' Jacko pushed himself up out of the chair.

Together they went back across the street to the sheriff's office. Cabot was just swallowing the last coffee in his cup when he saw them. He had seen enough of trouble to know when it was heading his way.

He got up quickly, and pushed back the chair so that it fell to the floor.

The noise startled Bert, who had been dozing in the back. He opened the door a mite and saw Cabot heading for the door.

'Hey,' he bawled at the retreating outlaw. 'You ain't paid for this stuff.'

Cabot kept on going. He snatched at the leathers. He jerked them free and jumped aboard.

Harris came running out of his office, his gun in his hand, watching Cabot rowelling the horse and heading down the dusty street. He tossed some lead after him, but it missed Cabot by yards. Cabot leathered his horse.

'Damn it, Jacko, git yer horse, an' we'll get after him,' Harris yelled.

Jacko ran towards the hitch rail along with Mitch. Harris got there a few seconds later.

Cabot lashed his horse as he went, leaving the hamlet behind him. He rode hard along the edge of a tree-lined gorge. Harris and the others were catching up with him, going hell for leather. He hauled his Winchester out of it's saddle holster, aimed at Cabot's back and fired. The horse that Cabot was riding leapt over a gopher hole at the last minute and instead of hitting Cabot in the back, between his shoulder blades, the bullet slammed into Cabot's shoulder, punching him over the neck of his horse.

Still conscious, he rolled clear of the animal's flailing hoofs, and fell into the gorge. His body rolled and rolled, slamming against the trees and rocks until it came to rest under the hoofs of Slade's horse.

TEN

Slade snatched on the leathers and dragged the frightened horse to a stop. He looked down from his saddle, and stared at Cabot for a minute. 'You're not hurt too badly.'

'Just who in hell's name are you?' Cabot demanded. He struggled to his feet.

'I'm the son of the fella you framed for a robbery,' Slade snarled, getting down from his horse.

'I've never set eyes on you or your pa,' Cabot said, his shoulder bleeding and his body aching from the rough ride.

Slade looked up at where Cabot had come from.

'I expect somebody was chasing you,' he said speculatively.

'You gonna turn me in to them?' Cabot asked.

'Not right now,' Slade told him. 'Maybe later.'

'Just who the hell are you?' Cabot asked him again, brushing off his clothes with his uninjured hand.

'I'm Jack Slade. Remember the stage my pa didn't rob, and how the mob lynched him for it.'

Cabot turned white.

'Don't worry, I ain't gonna kill you. I'll let the law decide what should be done with you,' said Slade.

'I'm a reformed character.' Cabot spoke with fear in his voice.

'I doubt it,' Slade laughed. 'Now get back on your horse and let's get out of here.'

'Ain't no way he could have survived a drop like that,' Sheriff Harris said to the other two as he took a step back from the edge of the gorge.

'Reckon not,' Mitch said disappointedly. 'That reward money could have come in real handy.'

'Seems like you're gonna have to keep on sweeping out the saloon, and the livery stable,' Harris said, putting his gun away.

The men mounted up and rode away.

Below them, masked by the trees and boulders, Cabot was heading towards Blake's Creek with Slade riding behind, holding his gun on him.

'It's gonna be a long slow walk from here,' Cabot said, massaging his burning shoulder.

'It'll do your soul good. Give you time to think about your misdeeds,' Slade answered.

'I've been thinkin' about my misdeeds. I was heading somewhere fresh to make a clean start.'

'You sound sincere,' Slade told him. 'But I

ain't too sure I can trust you.'

'Maybe you're right,' Cabot admitted. 'But ain't I deserving of a chance?'

Slade thought about it.

'Yeah, you're deserving of a chance,' he said slowly. 'But I'm still taking you back.'

'All right, you take me back, but there's a settlement a mile or so from here an' a fella owed me a favour. Maybe he'll lend me a horse fer a spell.'

Slade could see that Cabot was beginning to have some trouble walking, and he wasn't making such good time. If they kept going at this pace, they'd never get back to Blake's Creek. Not that he was in that much of a hurry, but he wanted to get there some day.

'OK, let's go see this fella,' he said to the back of Cabot's head.

'Thanks.' Cabot rubbed his bleeding shoulder.

They got to the place a couple of hours later.

'We ain't got no regular doctor, but we've got a fair horse-doctor,' Billy Grey said to Cabot when he had looked at his shoulder.

'Thanks, Billy. You just pass me a bottle of your best whiskey, an' I'll take it from there.'

Slade was in the front of Grey's cabin, eating some stew that Grey had fixed up for them both.

Slick Dillon had taken his boys out in the direction of the hamlet from which Cabot had ridden out.

'We ain't got time for the subtle stuff,' he said. 'We'll just go in and ask them, see what they say. He can't have got far and somebody might have caught a sight of him on the trail.' His men mounted up.

Harris was in his office, feeling disappointed and disgruntled when the gang rode down the only street in the hamlet. Straight away, he looked out of the window and saw the men. He grabbed his sixgun, jerked the door open and walked into the muzzle of Slick Dillon's shotgun. Dillon held it under his chin and edged him back into his office.

'Don't do anything that'll make me pull the trigger,' he said to the shaking Harris.

'OK,' Harris said as he started to sweat.

'We're trying to find a friend of ours. We got sorta separated. Wouldn't have happened to have seen him, would you?'

'What kinda man is he?' Harris asked him, his voice shaking.

'Kinda man you'd mistake fer a grizzly, if you were real short-sighted,' Dillon said with a laugh.

'He's bin through here,' Harris said, squinting at the shotgun.

'So where is he now?' Dillon poked him in the throat with the shotgun.

'He's dead. His horse threw him and he went over the side of Broken Neck Gorge.' Harris suddenly felt a mite easier when he saw the look in Dillon's face.

'You see the body?' Dillon asked suddenly.

'Me? Naw. I wasn't going down there.' Harris started squirming again.

'Maybe we'd best go and take a look,' Dillon smirked, jerking the shotgun away from Harris's throat.

'I ain't goin' down there. Why do you think it's called Broken Neck Gorge?' Harris felt sick all of a sudden.

'A big, brave lawman like you ain't afraid of a little thing like that,' Dillon said.

He grabbed Harris by the shirt front and hauled him outside. Most of the folks who lived in the hamlet had been mustered out in the street under the guns of Dillon's men.

'We're just gonna borrow your sheriff fer a while,' he shouted at them.

He got one of his boys to bring the sheriff's horse, and told Harris to get mounted. They rode out of the hamlet and along the trail to the place above Broken Neck Gorge where they had seen Cabot go over the edge.

'Did none of you boys go down to see if he was there?' Dillon asked the sheriff.

Harris shook his head nervously.

'Then I reckon you and me should go down, what do you say?' Dillon suggested. 'Marty, get a couple of ropes,' he called out to one of his men.

He got down and was handed two ropes.

Dillon tossed one to the sheriff.

'Get that fastened round yerself,' he ordered him, while doing the same with the one he had.

Harris did as he was bid.

'Now start climbing down,' Dillon indicated the lip of the gorge.

Nervously, Harris eased his way over the lip, and took a look down. Despite the intervening rocks and trees that blocked his view, he knew that Broken Neck Gorge was the hell of a drop.

'Start payin' out them ropes,' Dillon called as they began to work their way down the gorge.

Harris was pretty nervous. His fingers slid on the surface of the rocks sending down a shower of stones. The rope burned Harris's fingers as it ran through his hands. He shouted and Dillon laughed at the top of his voice. Above him some of his men echoed his laughter. Looking upwards Harris felt his stomach heave as his feet slipped against the surface of the gorge.

'Nearly there now, Sheriff,' Dillon laughed again. 'Just take a look down, there's nothin' to it.'

As he twisted his head to look at the ground, Harris felt sick.

'That's as far as the rope goes, boss,' a voice from above Harris called.

Harris twisted his head and looked up again. He could see an unshaven face grinning down at him.

'OK,' Dillon called back.

138

For a while he was silent.

'Can't see anything down there,' he shouted. 'Pull me up.'

'What about him?' the same voice called down.

'Get me up first,' Dillon answered.

He disappeared over the lip of the gorge, leaving Harris swinging in mid-air.

'See anything, boss?' one of his men asked when Dillon had taken off the rope.

'No, there ain't anybody down there.' Dillon took his knife out of its sheath at the back of his belt.

He cut the rope holding Harris. Harris screamed as he went down.

'If he ain't down there, then he's gone somewhere. We're gonna have to go all the way round and find him,' Dillon said as he got mounted.

They charged off down the twisting trail to the place where they picked up the tracks. The body of Harris twitched nearby in the sun.

'One of them is walking, boss,' Marty sang out from the edge of the trail.

'That's Cabot. Guess we'll find out who the other fella is when we catch up with them,' Dillon said.

Cabot persuaded Grey to lend him a horse, and he and Slade rode out.

'As soon as we get to Blake's Creek, I'm goin' to turn you over to a marshal, if I don't change my mind and shoot you first,' Slade told him, just to discourage any ideas Cabot might have of making a break for it.

'I told you, Slade, I'm a reformed character. Just give me an even chance, that's all,' Cabot said, rubbing his arm as he rode.

'You'll get as even a chance as my pa got from that lynch mob,' Slade told him.

For a spell they both fell silent. Then Slade caught sight of a rider approaching from down the trail.

'Clara,' he hailed her when she got within distance.

'Jack, it's Masters. He's killed his wife, and he knows you've come up here for him,' she said, nodding to Cabot.

'What does he want with me?' Cabot asked, already guessing the answer.

'Wanted to save Jack a job,' Clara said icily.

'You mean he's gonna kill me?' Cabot asked.

'Well, he ain't gonna send you to Sunday School,' Slade told him.

'You can't let him do that,' Cabot wailed.

'I'll do my damnedest,' Slade promised him. 'But maybe you're right, maybe I should leave it to a judge and jury. I've had to stop a lynching before, so I guess I must have known deep down I couldn't just kill you, no matter how I felt.'

'OK, but, I'll say anything you want.'

'The truth will do,' Slade snapped at him.

Masters had got back to his ranch, and was collecting the money from the safe in his ranch. As he put it in his saddle-bag it occurred to him that he need not pay Dillon the money at all. He grinned to himself then went into the yard.

'Bentine,' he called out, 'get some of the boys together, and get ready to head out.'

'Right, boss,' Bentine said, and went to get some of the boys.

Half an hour later they were heading up to Twin Bends.

Dillon and his boys were catching up on Slade and Clara.

Cabot had heard them coming a while back and his face had turned deathly white.

'If they catch me they'll kill me,' he kept on repeating.

'Then you'd best save your breath for riding, and just hope they don't catch up with you,' Clara snapped.

She was feeling as worried as Cabot. If they killed him, they'd sure as hell kill her and Slade.

Slade looked over his shoulder, and saw the first of them coming round a sharp bend in the trail. Drawing his .45 he started tossing some lead at them. Dillon was out in front. He put his .45 away, reached down to his saddle holster and hauled out his Winchester. He levered a round into the breech, aimed at Cabot's back and squeezed the trigger. The rifle kicked against his shoulder. Clara's horse stumbled and she was flung to the side of the trail, where she hit her head on a rock. Cabot was twisting his head to see how close their pursuers were when one of Dillon's boys fired at him. The shot went wide, but it gave Cabot more of a fright. He rowelled his horse even harder. Slade had seen Clara's horse go down, and hauled his own horse to a stop. A bullet hit the animal as he swung it round. As the creature went down, a bullet hit Slade in the shoulder and he fell out of the saddle.

'Leave them be,' Dillon yelled, seeing a couple of his boys aiming to stop. 'It's Cabot we want, not them.'

Cabot took a last glance over his shoulder, then kicked hard on his horse's flank.

'Hurry it up, boys,' Dillon yelled. 'He's getting away.'

Cabot looked over his shoulder again. The distance between him and Dillon was growing. He rowelled the horse viciously, and hung low over its neck. The lead was still coming over his shoulder, but not as near and not as often. The horse was in good shape and still had plenty of distance in him. He was starting to feel happier. Maybe he would make it. He laughed loudly, and patted the horse's neck.

The trail split off two ways. Cabot went left, hoping that the gang would lose some time before they picked it up again. The foliage was thickening out again, and he realized that it would become easier and easier to lose himself among the trees.

When Slade came to he wondered where he was, then it came back to him, along with the pain in his shoulder where the bullet had winged him. He got up and walked to where he could see Clara lying in the grass. A trickle of blood was running down her face and her head was bleeding a mite. He bent over her, took off his bandanna and wet it with water from her canteen. He cleaned her face and head with the water. After a few seconds her eyes started to open.

'What happened?' she asked him with a groan, feeling at her head.

'You took a fall. Are you hurt bad?'

'No, I don't think so,' she replied, looking at his arm. 'What about that?'

'I was lucky. It just scraped the flesh,' Slade told her, dabbing some water on the wound.

'Where's everybody else?' she asked, standing up.

'Dunno. I guess we're just gonna have to go and look for them,' answered Slade.

Cabot had ridden off the trail and was heading deeper and deeper into the trees and undergrowth. Having spent most of his life in this part of the country he reckoned he wouldn't have much trouble losing Dillon and his men. What he couldn't figure was how come he'd panicked and told Slade that he was a reformed man when a fortune in gold was within spitting distance. The loot from the Hanging Ridge railroad job. All in gold and just lying waiting for someone to come and pick it up. It would just fit nicely into his saddle-bags, he thought. All he had to do was to get there before Dillon figured out where he was heading. It was damn risky, he told himself, but that gold would set him up for life, and he wouldn't have to reform, he could just go on doing what he liked best, whoring and drinking whiskey.

In his eagerness to get to the gold, he let the branches of the trees scratch at his face, leaving bloody scratch marks down his cheeks. He bent low in the saddle to try to avoid them. It was a good distance to the place where they'd hidden the gold, and he couldn't see Dillon catching up with him. He'd never rated Slade, even as a kid, when they'd strung his old man up. Slade had just got lucky. Cabot laughed as he recalled old man Slade being dragged from that jail and strung up on the tree outside. All for a few acres of land that Masters wanted.

Well, it was all in the past now, all he had to do was pick up the gold and ride away.

Cabot rode on until he found the stream with the two trees leaning over it, their branches tangled up. He dismounted and moved along the banks of the stream, his hand not far from his gun, despite the fact that he didn't think there would be anybody around. The stream curved a few yards from where he had left his horse. Getting down on one knee, he pulled up the sleeve of his shirt and reached down into the water. Its coldness took his breath away. His fingers moved around the bank, until they came to the sharp rock, and then the leather strap holding the bag with the gold in it.

A grin of pleasure crossed his features as he hauled on the leather until the worn bag broke the surface. The water drained off it as he tore at the strap and opened it up. The yellow metal coins spilled on to the ground, shining in the sunlight. He grinned greedily.

Cabot refastened the strap of the bag and carried it over to his horse. It was still dripping as he fastened it to his saddle pommel, and turned to ride away.

Dillon watched him from the cover of the undergrowth.

'Thanks, Cabot, you son-of-a-bitch,' he said. He levered a round into the breech of the Winchester and raised the gun to his shoulder.

Cabot felt nothing but sudden rising of the hairs on the back of his neck a second before the bullet hit him and pitched him into the water.

Dillon got up, feeling pretty well satisfied with himself, and waited for the rest of his boys to catch up with him.

They walked through the undergrowth to the river's edge. Cabot's blood was turning the water red as it swirled downstream. Dillon cut the bag from the pommel.

'Let's get back and collect from Masters,' he said, jocularly.

They tramped back to their horses and set out.

ELEVEN

Slade and Clara hadn't much trouble following the trail.

'We're just gonna have to keep following them until we know where they're heading,' Slade said.

'Got any bright ideas where that might be?' Clara asked, wiping the sweat out of her eyes.

'No, but they must be following Cabot for a reason.' He swiped at the flies that were trying to lick at the blood on his face.

They trudged on following the hoof marks in the dust. Slade heard a sound.

'Best get off the trail,' he said, grabbing Clara by her arm and pulling her into the long grass. He hauled out his .45.

Seconds later Dillon and the rest of his men rode by.

Slade waited until they had ridden past and then looked up.

'I reckon they're gone by now,' he said.

'That means you can get off me,' Clara said to him.

Slade looked down. 'You sure are pretty,' he said, with a grin.

Clara's eyebrows furrowed. Slade kissed her.

'We'd better be getting on,' he said standing up.

'Do we have to?' Clara asked with a breathless smile, touching her lips where he had kissed her.

' 'Fraid so. It looks like they've caught up with Cabot. Didn't notice the horse he was riding, though. If we found it it would make things a lot easier,' said Slade.

They started off down the trail again, watching the hoof marks.

'It ain't getting any easier,' Slade said as they went into the undergrowth.

'Look.' Clara suddenly pointed to the horse that Cabot had been riding. It was chomping contendly on the grass beside Cabot's body.

They moved cautiously forward for fear of spooking it. When they had got close to it, Slade grabbed the leathers, and stroked its muzzle to calm it down.

'There's something over there, just by the river bank,' Clara said excitedly.

They both went over to where Cabot's body lay, his arms hanging over the river into the water.

'It's Cabot.' Slade pulled Cabot's head up out of the water.

'Well, at least we got a horse,' Clara said.

'Doesn't help me much, does it?' Slade said.

'I guess not,' Clara sat down on the bank of the river. 'Got any bright ideas?'

'Not right off,' Slade ruminated, sitting beside her. 'The best thing to do is follow them and see what they're up to.'

He kicked the horse's flanks and pointed him in the direction of where they had last seen Dillon and his gang. Within a couple of hours they were catching up with them.

Masters and Bentine were leading the hunt in the opposite direction.

'OK, Bentine,' Masters said, throwing up his hand to halt his men. 'I'll just follow the river and go under the waterfall, an' give Slick his money. Then we ride in and get my money back.'

'What about Cabot?' Bentine asked him.

Masters shrugged. 'What about him? He'll be staying there one way or the other.'

'OK,' Bentine said as Masters disappeared along the river.

Masters rode under the waterfall, the water drowning out the sound of his horse.

From somewhere up ahead a voice called out to him to halt. 'It's me, Masters,' he called back.

One of Dillon's men came out of the gloom of the cave.

'You'd better get up there,' he saved waving Masters on.

'Thanks, I'm obliged,' Masters said.

Dillon and the others were in the cabin drinking and playing cards when Masters walked in.

Masters took the saddle-bag from his horse, slung it over his shoulder and went inside.

'You got the money?' Dillon asked him, without looking up from the cards.

'Yeah, I got the money,' Masters said, dropping the saddle-bag on the floor. Dillon folded his hand and picked up the saddle-bag. The others watched as he spread the wad of bills on the table. They let out a low whistle as Dillon picked up one of the wads and rifled it.

'You've got your money. Now where's Cabot?' Masters asked.

'Cabot's saying hello to the fishes,' Dillon laughed easily. 'We left him face down in the stream, where we stashed the haul from the railroad job. He's dead all right.'

'OK,' Masters said with a feeling of confidence.

'You want to go back and take a look?' Dillon's voice was hard.

'No, I guess I'll take your word for it,' Masters replied.

'Guess you will,' Dillon said. He dropped the wad back on to the table.

Masters looked at him and the others. 'Guess we're done, then,' he said.

Dillon looked at him. 'I guess we are.'

Masters turned and headed for the door.

'Be seein' you,' Dillon called out to him as he went through the door.

'Be seeing' you,' Masters called back.

Outside Masters climbed into the saddle and headed back through the waterfall.

'They in there?' Bentine asked him when they met up.

'Yeah, they're in there,' Masters told him.

'Then what are we waiting for?' Bentine raised his hand and urging the men on.

They galloped through the waterfall and out the other side into the cave.

As they came one of Dillon's men saw them and yelled a warning. Nobody in the cabin heard it until the first shots hit the woodwork.

'It's that double-crossing, Masters,' Dillon yelled just before he slammed the door shut against a hail of lead.

His men in the cabin started to tear down the cloth where the windows should have been and send back some lead.

'Come on, Slick, all I want is my money,' Masters yelled over the sound of the gunfire.

'Then you come and you take it,' Dillon called back.

'If you say so,' Masters shouted to him. 'Be right over for it any time now.'

Dillon and his boys were taking a licking. Dillon had taken some lead in the arm and a couple of his boys had taken some in the head.

'Come on, Slick. There's no reason for you all

to die. Just toss out the money and we'll go away.'

'The hell you will,' Dillon hollered back, tight-ening his blood-soaked bandanna over his mashed arm, his face a mask of rage and hatred.

'What are we gonna do, boss?' one of his boys called over.

'I'm working on it,' Dillon ground out, as he bit back the pain.

'Just make it quick, that's all,' the voice called back to him.

'Yeah, OK,' Dillon told him.

He thought hard as the pain in his arm wors-ened.

The wood above his head splintered as a .45 shell slammed into it. Dillon cursed and tossed some lead back from where the shell had come. A wreath of smoke curled down from the roof. He looked up at it.

'The bastards are trying to burn us out,' one of his boys screamed as a burning timber crashed into the cabin, setting fire to his clothes.

Dillon glanced over his shoulder.

'OK, boys,' he shouted. 'Just shoot yer way out. Every man for himself.'

The men left in the cabin got to their feet and ran for the door, firing as they went. Outside, Masters, Bentine and the rest of them waited, guessing what was coming.

'Here they come,' Masters called out, raising his .45 to fire as the door burst open and Dillon's men tumbled out into the gunfire. One by one,

Dillon's men went over clutching their last bullet wound.

Inside the burning cabin, Dillon waited for the ruckus to subside. Through the blinding smoke, he crawled to the door nursing his injured arm. Easing the door open he squinted through the crack. Most of his boys were down and Masters' men were finishing off the others. He grabbed the saddle-bag, slipped outside while Masters' boys were checking the bodies, and finished off those who weren't quite dead. Masters picked up the saddle-bag with his money in it, and slung it over his shoulder. When he reached the end of the cabin, he moved round the corner and out of sight. Dillon moved along the back of the cabin, keeping it between him and Masters' boys. The inside of the cave was lit by the flames from the cabin.

As he got to the back wall a chunk of lead from a .45 chipped the rock above his head and he heard somebody call out. Another piece of lead slammed into the rock and he heard the sound of running footsteps.

'There he is,' Masters called out.

Dillon ran like hell, watching all the time where he was going. He started to move round in a semicircle, moving closer and closer to where Masters and his boys had left their horses. The men holding them turned at the sound of the ruckus and took a shot at Masters. The shot went wide. Masters threw one back. A man clutched his chest and fell. Masters picked out a black horse, grabbed it by the leathers and swung himself up into the saddle. As he rowelled its flanks he fired a couple of shots into the air and stampeded the rest of the horses. The animals galloped down the trail with Masters behind them. He splashed through the water and came out into the sunlight.

When he got out Masters let out a whoop. He was free and clear. A few minutes later Bentine and his boys came out.

'Got it,' he yelled slapping the saddle-bag.

'OK, boss.' Bentine laughed, riding up alongside him.

'Like I said, I'm getting out of the territory for a spell. You and these boys go back to the ranch. The law hasn't got nothing on you.'

'Where'll you be?' Bentine asked.

'I ain't rightly sure,' Masters told him. 'I'll get word to you.'

Bentine watched him ride away.

'Reckon we'll be seein' that fella again?' Mather asked him.

Slowly, his hand reaching for the stock of his carbine, Bentine shook his head.

'Reckon not,' he said, as he levered a round into the breech. He raised the rifle to his shoulder and squeezed the trigger. Masters leaped out of the saddle as the piece of lead hit him between the shoulder blades.

'That saddle-bag of his sure looks heavy,'

Mather said as he rode up to where Masters lay.

Bentine slid his rifle into his saddle holster.

'I was just thinkin the same thing,' Bentine said. He climbed out and reached up to Masters' saddle-bag. He hauled it down, pulled it open and looked inside. Mather watched Bentine's eyes open wide and heard him give a low whistle.

'What is it?' he demanded. He climbed out of the saddle and took the bag from Bentine's hands.

'The rat was aiming to run out on us with this,' he said.

'Sure looks like it,' Bentine laughed. 'Musta bin the haul from one of the jobs they pulled. He sure ain't going to need it now.'

'No, but we can sure use it now we're out of a job,' Mather laughed. 'We'd best be going before the others catch up with us,' he added, going for his horse.

As he did so, Bentine pulled his .45 and shot him in the back.

'Wrong,' he said, putting his gun away. 'I need it.'

He climbed aboard and headed down the trail.

Slade and Clare saw Bentine coming towards them. They hauled off the trail and waited for him to draw level with them. Then Slade rode out, his gun in his hand.

'Hold it, Bentine,' he called out.

Bentine kept going, but Slade put a bullet in the air.

'I said hold it,' he called again.

Bentine threw up his hands. Slade rode round to the front of him.

'If it ain't the fella from the saloon,' Bentine smirked. 'I ain't got anything you want.'

'I want Masters,' Slade told him.

Bentine laughed out loud.

'What's so funny?' Slade asked him.

'They're both dead. Masters and Dillon.'

'Both dead?' Slade echoed. 'Cabot?'

'Seems like we've got an echo out here.' Bentine laughed again. 'Them and Cabot. Deader than the rats they were.' Bentine was watching Slade carefully.

The news had taken Slade by surprise, and he lowered his gun a mite. Bentine made a dive for his, but Slade recovered himself and shot him. As Bentine fell from the saddle Slade dismounted and ran over to him.

'Did Cabot say anything about a stage robbery?' Slade asked the wounded outlaw.

For a minute Bentine hesitated.

'I don't know how much good it'll do you in court, but it might do you some,' Slade said, seeing Bentine's hesitation.

'Yeah, OK,' Bentine said finally. 'Him and Masters cooked it up so Masters could get your pa's land. Leastways that's what he told me.'

'You willing to tell that to a US marshal?' Slade

asked him. 'It might save you from hanging.'

'I guess so,' Bentine said in a beaten way. 'There's something else as well. There's some gold from one of their robberies in that saddle-bag. Not a heist that I was on. It might do me some good if you take it back.' He nodded in the direction of his horse.

Clara took the gold from the saddle-bag.

'He's damn right,' she laughed, showing Slade some of the gold.

'Let's get going,' Slade said, pushing Bentine up into the saddle.